C000321252

"Beck," she whispered. "Please try to understand."

He took hold of her neck and drew her closer to him. "Understand what? That you ran away from me?"

"I didn't run away. My mother sent me." She covered his mouth with a cold hand. Tears glimmered in her eyes. "Beck, I was pregnant."

He swept her hand away and rose up onto his elbows, a sucker punch pummeling his chest. "Pregnant?"

She nodded as tears glistened and flowed over her lids.

"Why didn't you tell me?" He shot up to sit. "We could have worked something out. I had plans for us."

"You don't understand."

A torrent of mixed-up feelings swept over him—anger, grief, frustration—they swirled together, making him queasy. He jumped off the bed, fought for balance and set off pacing the floor. "You were pregnant with my child and you didn't tell me?" He bit back the wave of nausea that pressed against his stomach and threatened to move up his throat. "How could you not tell me?"

Dear Reader

When I sat down to write this book, TEMPORARY DOCTOR, SURPRISE FATHER, I had the image of a formerly bubbly, beautiful young woman, who had changed drastically in the thirteen years since she'd met and fallen in love with her high-school sweetheart. He'd left for boot camp, been chosen for Special Forces, become a Green Beret medic, travelled the world, and carried on with his life. She'd made a painful decision, harboured a huge secret, and paid a devastatingly emotional price. And it had changed her life. The choices we make in our youth often come back to haunt us.

As this reunion story unfolds, I hope you'll fall in love with my gorgeous hero, Beck, as much as I did. And I suspect, once you've scratched the gruff exterior of my heroine, January, you'll want to be friends with her.

A bit about Special Forces medics here. They are first on scene in the battlefield, and what they do for the injured can save lives. Their training is intense, and in all my years in nursing I haven't come close to doing many of the procedures our medics learn in their Special Forces training. Hats off to those who volunteer for this difficult job. There is only one word to describe them. Heroes!

I love to hear from readers. If I've struck a chord with you in this book, let me know. Or if you'd just like to say hello, you can visit me at my website: www.lynnemarshallweb.com. And if you enjoy blogs, a group of us Medical™ Romance authors have got together for *Love is the Best Medicine*, a blog which we update every week. You can link to it from my website.

Thanks for reading my book!

L

TEMPORARY DOCTOR, SURPRISE FATHER

BY
LYNNE MARSHALL

MILLS & BOON®
Pure reading pleasure™

First published in Great Britain 2009
Harlequin Mills & Boon Limited,
Eton House, 18-24 Paradise Road, Richmond, Surrey TW9 1SR

© Lynne Marshall 2009

ISBN: 978 0 263 20922 8

Set in Times Roman 10½ on 12¾ pt
15-0409-48659

Printed and bound in Great Britain
by CPI Antony Rowe, Chippenham, Wiltshire

Lynne Marshall has been a registered nurse in a large California hospital for twenty-five years. She has now taken the leap to writing full time, but still volunteers at her local community hospital. After writing the book of her heart in 2000, she discovered the wonderful world of Medical™ Romance, where she feels the freedom to write the stories she loves. She is happily married, has two fantastic grown children, and a socially challenged rescued dog. Besides her passion for writing Medical™ Romance, she loves to travel and read. Thanks to the family dog, she takes long walks every day!

Recent titles by the same author:

ASSIGNMENT: BABY
PREGNANT NURSE, NEW-FOUND FAMILY
SINGLE DAD, NURSE BRIDE

This book is dedicated with love
to the only Special Forces medic I know—
my son the Green Beret, John-Philip.

PROLOGUE

"WILL you wait for me?" Beck Braxton wove his fingers through January Stewart's long platinum hair to frame her face. Standing in the driveway of her house, she avoided his eyes. "Will you?"

She gave a reluctant nod.

"I love you. You know that," he said, wishing they were somewhere much more private.

Tears brimmed and gathered on her thick lashes. "Then why are you leaving?" Her voice quivered.

He bit his lip to push back his brewing frustration. "We've gone over this a thousand times, January. I've got to get out of here. When I come back things will be different. I promise."

She blinked and tears zigzagged down her cheeks. The light from the streetlamp made them glow.

"Tell me you love me." He was leaving for army boot-camp early next morning, and though she'd said it a hundred times before, he needed to hear it again. Now.

"You know I love you," she mumbled, fisting his shirt and pulling on it in a desperate gesture.

This wasn't at all like the gorgeous and confident girl he knew.

She pulled him near and he kissed her, tears mixing with their kiss. Salt and sadness tainted their goodbye. God, he hated this. He didn't want to leave her any more than she wanted him to leave, but it was time to set out on his own. He was only eighteen. If he wanted to be a man and marry the woman he loved, he'd have to suck it up and follow the only path he knew.

He'd dreamed of joining the army since the age of twelve, anything to get away from his father and a dead-end future in Atwater. As he'd grown older, he'd fantasized about adventure and seeing the world. He'd started hanging out at the army recruiter's office when he'd first gotten his driver's license at sixteen. They knew him by name and had fed his dreams with their own stories of military service. He'd signed up as soon as he could at seventeen, knowing he'd have to wait until he was eighteen and after he graduated from high school before he could officially join.

Then he'd met January last year, and had fallen in love for the first time in his life. Fallen. In. Love. Big time.

He'd walked across the auditorium stage last night and accepted his high-school diploma. She'd been in the audience, being a year behind. Leaving was the hardest thing he'd ever had to do, but he hoped she'd understand and everything would work out. He'd come back as soon as he could to marry her and take her with him, wherever he was stationed. But he couldn't tell her that just yet, not until he'd worked everything out.

"Promise you'll wait for me," he whispered over her lips.

"I…"

"January!" her mother's shrill voice called from the porch.

CHAPTER ONE

IF JANUARY Ashworth saw one more couple making out, she'd scream. Was it mating season or something? The young ortho tech and his nurse girlfriend were wrapped so close together it was hard to figure out where one left off and the other began. On the drive into work she'd seen two teenagers at a bus stop with their hands all over each other—she'd almost beeped her horn to break them up—and now this. And why, at one month shy of thirty, did she feel so old?

Running late, she pulled into a free spot and parked. After grabbing the pile of mail from the front seat, which she'd picked up on her way out of her house, she slammed the car door. Jan turned to see if the racket had fazed the lovebirds as they continued to lock lips. It hadn't. Wasn't there a rule about necking in the Los Angeles Mercy Hospital employee parking lot?

Jan shook her head, adjusted her glasses and, in the hope of getting the vision of lust out of her mind, glanced toward the afternoon sun. It only made her sneeze. Not even that got their attention. When had she last been kissed so passionately? Refusing to go there, she shook her head again and wiped her itching nose with a tissue.

Five minutes later, after zipping her name badge through the time-clock machine, she headed toward the emergency department while sorting through her mail. The newspaper said there'd be a full moon tonight, and it was Friday on top of that. Between the old ER tale of the full moon bringing out the medical crazies and the guaranteed usual Friday-night crowd, she knew it would be extra-busy tonight. And if her continued sneezing and watery eyes were any indication, a cold was brewing.

Things were not looking good…until she spied one special letter in the pile of mail. She recognized the address and got a warm, achy feeling in her heart, then promptly slipped it inside her scrub pocket to savor later.

Carmen Estrada, the no-nonsense ER charge nurse, waved her over the second her crepe-soled shoes hit the threshold. "Jan! I wanted to clue you in on a decision Dr. Riordan has made and already implemented." The tall, middle-aged woman gave her a once-over. "Have you been crying? Your nose is red."

"Sneezing." Jan slipped an oversized nondescript-color OR gown over her loose scrubs as she studied the unnatural black hair of her supervisor. "So what's up?" She nodded and listened distractedly.

"We'll be accommodating a National Guard medic over the next month. He's gearing up for another tour of duty and needs a quickie skills refresher course. He'll be working under the umbrella of Dr. Riordan's license and the agreement the hospital made with the National Guard. Any stitches, broken bones, chest tubes, intubations, gunshot wounds—you catch my drift—make sure the medic gets first dibs."

Still distracted, rather than tying the straps of the OR gown, Jan stuffed them in her pocket with the letter. "What about the interns and residents? Aren't they going to gripe?"

"Sure they are, but Gavin doesn't give a patootie about that. He wants the medic to get first dibs."

Jan inhaled and held her breath. She and Carmen exchanged knowing looks. No need to protest, the king of the ER had spoken. Once Gavin Riordan made up his mind about anything, it became emergency department law.

"Whatever," Jan finally said on an exhalation.

Carmen used her high forehead as if it was a beacon light and nodded toward Dr. Riordan's open office. A tall, fit-looking man in a police uniform with sculpted arms and a nearly shaved head was shaking hands with Dr. Riordan. Surprising and unwanted humming vibrated over the nerve endings in her spine. What was it about a man in a uniform?

The hair rose on the back of Jan's neck as she went on alert. There was something about that profile, the line of his shoulders, his stance that put her on edge. "I thought you said he's with the National Guard. That guy's a cop."

"He's on the LAPD SWAT team, is a Special Forces trained medic, and also is on the National Guard, so I'm told."

"Impressive. How can he work here and on the force at the same time?"

"He's coming in on his days off and after hours."

Some sixth sense sent a rush of blood from her suddenly pounding heart, making her cheeks get hot. She forced herself to act nonchalant. "Sounds pretty dedicated."

"From what Gavin says, the guy's proved himself through several tours of duty and is gearing up for another."

At three-quarter view, a sharp brow line, deep-set, appraising eyes and a straight profile began to fill in the blanks on the missing person's report in her head. Though his hair was closely cropped, the stubble looked dark. Almost black. Just like…

"Hmm. So when does he start?"

"Right now."

With her eyes darting around the ED for places to hide—not that she was positive she knew him or anything, mostly it was an eerie feeling the mysterious cop dragged out of her—Jan made an about-face, planning to slink away and skulk in the background for the rest of her shift.

"Jan?" Gavin called her name, and any hope of keeping a low profile trickled away.

She adjusted her glasses and attempted to swallow a wad of cotton wedged in her throat as she went on guard, hoping the man wouldn't recognize her, and turned. "Yes?"

Gavin swaggered across the room, steering along the newest addition to the ED. "This is Officer Beck Braxton."

After a mini-implosion in her chest—it was him!—Jan nodded a cautious greeting and worked to conceal the unnerving reaction fizzing through her body. She didn't offer to shake his hand. She couldn't. Beck gave her a stealthy once-over, his mouth thinning into a polite straight line.

"He's a highly trained field medic and needs to update his trauma skills. You've got your PA license, haven't you, Beck?"

Beck shook his head. "Actually, I never got round to it before I joined SWAT." So Beck had been a military field medic who was now a police officer on the special weapons and tactics team. Who would ever have thought?

"That's a shame because, from what I've heard, you've got the knack." Gavin shifted back to Jan. "I've already told him what a great nurse you are." In a subversively charming way, Gavin smiled. He wasn't kidding anyone, least of all her. He was merely blowing smoke up her stethoscope to soften her up before he dropped the bomb. "You'll be assisting him tonight."

Gulp. She fought back a cough. No way could she work with him.

"Wherever he goes, whatever he needs, you see to it he gets it. I've seen Beck work. He doesn't need me breathing down his neck unless something big comes in."

Dark brown hair, pale skin, lips ripe for kissing, hazel eyes that could make a girl do something she'd never planned—a face she'd never thought she'd see again.

Her mind drifted back to the couple in the parking lot. The last time she'd been swept off her feet by a kiss had been with Beck. A quick memory popped into her head of how her knees had buckled the first time he'd kissed her, and how he'd had to hold her up by backing her against the lockers in the school hallway. Standing before her was something much more disturbing than the high-school version. Beck had grown into a mature and dangerously attractive man, though he didn't act as though he knew it.

Her stomach backflipped and stuck the landing with a quick punch of pain.

"Got it?" Gavin challenged.

Jan prayed that thirteen years, a name change, and an extreme make-over might throw Beck off her trail. No longer January Stewart, the popular high-school prom queen, now she was a once-divorced, radically toned-down version of her former self. Everything about her was different, from her last name to bobbed dark blond hair instead of long brash platinum waves cupping her waist. She wore glasses now instead of contacts, and had gained a handful of strategically placed pounds. He really shouldn't recognize her. Should he?

"Got it," she mumbled, wiping her nose with a tissue to disguise her face, her voice sounding gravelly from her tickling throat.

"Thanks," Beck said. "And it's nice to meet you." Something flickered in his eyes when he reached for and shook her other hand. Recalling how his eye color could change from day to day depending on what he wore, she quickly looked away before her warming cheeks became too obvious, but not before she'd already noticed they were gray-blue today. His hand felt calloused, as if he was no stranger to hard work. That made sense for the street tough kid who'd always longed for adventure. Legions of awakening nerve endings marched up from her hand to her arm and fanned out across her shoulders.

A fond memory of how secure she'd once felt holding his hand flashed into her mind. She loosened her grip and let her hand slip free, anything to stop the reaction, but her mind refused to shut down.

Never in a million years would she ever have guessed he'd become a police officer. He'd done everything in his power to act like an outlaw in his teens, always getting into fights and not caring what anyone, including teachers, had to say.

Her lips tickled at the edges with the absurdity. But he'd never have dreamed she'd become a nurse, either. "Most likely to be a movie star." Wasn't that what her high-school annual had predicted for her? Heck, they'd even inserted a pair of sunglasses over one of her rare candid pictures with the caption, "Bright future. Must wear shades."

Carmen strode around the ER desk and plopped a clipboard in Gavin's hand. "Full moon's apparently already rising. We've got a level-one trauma in transit. A gunshot wound. ETA five minutes," she said with her usual aplomb.

Grateful for the distraction, Jan went on alert.

"Is this gang related?" Dr. Riordan asked.

"Not sure, but he fits the age range and the neighborhood."

"Notify Security and lock down the ED waiting room just in case."

"Already have," Carmen retorted.

Gavin lifted his brows, tilted his head and trained his dark eyes on Beck. "Are you off duty yet?"

"Just about."

"Then you'd better get changed."

Adrenaline pumped through every vein in Beck's body in the men's locker room. Wasn't that what he lived for? The mention of a gunshot wound sent his mind spiraling back to his last tour of duty. Though gunshot wounds had been common, they had been the least of his worries then. What still haunted him were IEDs—improvised explosive devices—and lost body parts and burns, plus the fact you could never easily identify the difference between the enemy and the local allies. To this day he tensed whenever he passed an abandoned car at the side of the road.

Beck forced himself to focus on the job at hand. He'd learned that was all he could ever do. *Think of it as another adventure. One more for the file.*

Something else butted into his thinking. Why did that

nurse seem so familiar? She wasn't exactly his type, but an odd current had traveled up his arm when they'd shaken hands. She hadn't looked him in the eyes, and with lightly tinted glasses like those, it had been hard to read her expression. She'd seemed to squirm, and it surprised him. Usually, women reacted much more welcomingly to his touch. He shook his head. He should be focusing on the incoming GSW, yet…there was something *very* familiar about her.

After stripping and throwing on a pair of thread-worn scrubs, he realized he only had his work boots for shoes. Looking around the room, he spotted some extra-large OR shoe covers and slipped them on over his boots. Tucking in and tying the waistband on his scrubs, he rushed toward Gavin Riordan, the man offering his ER and saving him three weeks' intensive training in North Carolina. Along with everyone else, he waited at the ambulance entrance for hell to break loose as they all applied personal protective gear.

And there she was again, the nurse, waiting beside Gavin. Her height and oval-shaped face definitely reminded him of his high-school sweetheart. Some sweetheart she'd turned out to be. No sooner had he left for bootcamp then she'd torn his heart out of his chest and stomped on it. Focus, Braxton, focus.

One thing struck him about the ER: it was so much quieter here than in the field. Then, boom, the ambulance entrance doors flew open, and Gavin and the trauma team jumped into action around the gurney.

"Got the call a half hour ago," the first EMT said.

"It's a penetrating injury. Gunshot wound to right chest wall with possible pneumothorax," the second EMT said, while assisting the semi-conscious young patient's breathing with an ambubag as the team rolled the stretcher down the hall.

Beck remembered the term "the golden hour", the most important sixty minutes in any trauma patient's life if he was to survive. Though things might look chaotic, there was, in fact, a planned system by the attending doctor and his team for checking the ABCs—airway, breathing, circulation—and making primary and secondary surveys of the patient.

"No other obvious injuries noted." The EMT gave them the run-down of vital signs and initial assessment while they made their way down the corridor. "A 16-gauge IV placed in left forearm, infusing normal saline at 150 cc per hr. Pressure dressing applied to point of entry wound."

Bright motion-activated lighting snapped on the moment they crossed the threshold of the trauma room, illuminating all the gory details. Wine-colored blood covered most of the victim's clothes. A C-collar had been applied at the scene as he'd fallen out of a truck. They'd attempted to relieve the apparent tension pneumothorax with a needle at the second rib below the collarbone. It may have saved the guy's life.

On the count of three the team transferred the patient to the larger procedure room bed.

The familiar-looking nurse with the boxy glasses and shy attitude went right to work cutting off the patient's clothes, using surprising force to rip the shirtsleeves open to speed up the process. Even her mannerisms reminded him of January. But she'd had so much more style than this woman. She had been bubbly and full of life. This woman seemed subdued and almost beaten down. But they called her Jan. Hmm. Could thirteen years change someone that much?

A chaotic dance ensued among two doctors and three nurses. Their hands and bodies worked together, stepping aside, sliding under, reaching over, around, and through to get an airway placed, the patient hooked up to monitors, and a second IV started.

Beck wasn't sure whether to hold off or jump right in with the team, but followed his gut and helped Jan remove every last stitch of clothing and toss it to the floor. He kicked the wad of clothes at his feet toward the wall to prevent anyone from tripping on it.

Gavin gave instruction that the OR be notified then called out a list of orders, including labs, blood gases, X-rays and two units of blood, while he did what Beck remembered as the primary survey. It was a methodical approach to checking the airway, breathing and circulation. Gavin auscultated the patient's lungs and mumbled, "Crepitus" then studied the wound more closely. "Luckily for him this bullet nicked a vein and not an artery," he said, palpating the femoral artery on the same side before he uncovered another gunshot wound lower down the leg.

The patient's cold, clammy skin made Beck suspect shock.

"Get me a chest tube drain with autotransfusion," Gavin told the nurse beside him.

Beck knew that meant Gavin suspected hemothorax—blood surrounding the lung instead of air. Beneath the first-aid bandages applied at the scene, a quarter-sized crater erupting with thick dark blood was located in the right upper quadrant and became the center of attention. Until the lungs were stabilized, the second, less threatening gunshot wound could wait.

The overhead monitor alarm beeped rapidly as the initial

vital signs registered. The oxygen sats had tanked, BP was 80/40 and the pulse 130. The youth's heart was working like crazy in an attempt to maintain his body's circulation, and with a pneumothorax his lungs weren't getting nearly enough oxygen. If not stopped, it would be a deadly cycle.

"Let's get that chest tube in now," Gavin said, searching for and finding Beck. Their eyes met in wordless communication, and Gavin stepped back, allowing Beck to approach the man. Baptism by fire.

Jan magically reappeared and rolled over a tray with all the equipment he'd need. He flashed back to his training, then several tours of duty, and recalled each step of the process of inserting a chest tube. He'd done his share of them in the field. Feeling under a microscope here, with the world watching, he donned sterile gloves and, driven by adrenaline, hoped his hands didn't shake too noticeably.

After prepping the skin with antiseptic, he draped it with a sterile towel. He palpated the space between the fifth and sixth ribs and reached for the large syringe Jan handed him. He inserted the needle into the bottle of lidocaine she held for him, and administered the local anesthetic, waited briefly then accepted the proffered scalpel and made an incision in the mid-axillary line. She dutifully handed him a sterile package she'd begun to open from the outside, which gave easy access to the inside tubing without contaminating it.

Beck glanced briefly into her eyes just before he took it. For one beat their gazes locked. At close range, her eyes were blue, just like January's. Damn.

A mini-jolt of adrenaline helped him refocus. Using the rigid guide, he inserted the tube into the pleural cavity and aimed upwards as he slowly advanced it until he felt resistance. He pulled back a tiny bit and clamped the tube. With no sign of blood, the wounded young man had been lucky. Jan connected the tube to an underwater seal before he undid the clamp. A reassuring bubbling sound gave him the confidence to begin suturing the tube in place. Soon, with the trapped air removed and no longer pressing against the lung, the lung could reinflate and the man would be breathing a lot easier.

"OK, let's get a chest X-ray to check positioning," Gavin said as he clamped a hand on Beck's shoulder. "Good job."

To say Beck wasn't relieved would be lying, but the knowledge of a job well done admittedly felt good. "Thanks. It's been a while."

Jan wrapped adhesive tape around the tube and affixed it to the patient's chest wall, then Beck looped the chest tube and taped it snugly to the patient's abdomen before applying the final dressing.

Once Beck stepped back after his part was finished, Gavin took over. He'd located the superficially lodged bullet and removed it, then plopped it into a plastic specimen container held by Jan.

"Fantastical," she mumbled as she studied the bloody ball of metal while Gavin stabilized the patient and readied him for surgery.

Had she just said *fantastical*? That was it. The missing link. In the midst of chaos and saving a life, quick memories popped into his mind of the only other person he'd ever heard say "fantastic" that way. If he hadn't been sure before, he definitely was now.

But this person was nothing like that girl.

Still reeling from the notion that he'd stumbled on his first love, he watched Gavin proceed with a secondary survey head-to-toe assessment for more subtle injuries.

While consciously avoiding any thoughts about his ex-girlfriend, he waited for the chest X-ray films. Beck leaned against the wall and observed the team hovering over the patient, whose vital signs were already improving. He lifted the protective goggles from his eyes where perspiration had started to bead and steam them up, resting the glasses on his forehead. He glanced around the gurney from person to person, with everyone intent on what they were doing. Excellent teamwork.

Beck noticed a second pile of discarded clothing on the floor next to Jan's feet. He moved to kick it aside and couldn't help but notice something out of character for the subdued nurse. Completely out of place on her seriously sensible shoes were bright pink satin laces. A telltale sign of who she really was. So she hadn't dumped all her flash. His gaze traveled up to her face carefully hidden behind dark, thick-framed artsy glasses. He looked more closely. Her eyes were as bright a blue as they had been thirteen years ago.

How had he not recognized her mouth right off? In high school she'd carefully outlined those soft, well-shaped lips with liner before she'd applied the brightest shades of pink he'd ever seen. It had driven him crazy. She was the last person in the world he'd ever expected to run into here.

For a woman who wrapped herself in the loosest scrubs possible, it was hard to imagine her as once dressing like a birthday present in loud patterns over a curvaceous figure. Short skirts had never looked better than over those legs. But today her legs were covered in baggy, faded scrubs, making it impossible to compare. Yet there *were* those pink satin laces shining up at him. And she *had* said "fantastical".

It all added up to one person. January. And he was still as mad as hell at her.

She caught him looking at her and quickly glanced away. Could she tell that he'd just figured out who she was? Years before, she'd trampled over his heart without so much as a backward glance. He'd joined the army intent on seeing the world and had expected her to wait for him. Maybe it had been a lame plan, but it had been the best he could come up with at eighteen. When he'd gotten out of bootcamp, she'd disappeared. When he'd tracked her down, she'd broken up with him. Over the phone!

The skittish nurse shoved something toward him. He jumped back from sorting through memories to the present. She gave him a kit, avoiding his eyes. It was a Foley catheter kit.

"Make yourself useful," Jan said, jabbing the plastic-covered box at him then quickly turning away.

He glanced at the naked patient lying on the gurney. The young man was in and out of consciousness, and Beck hoped when he catheterized him, for the patient's sake, he'd be out of it.

As he opened the sterile package and started to set up, he glanced back at Jan, who was completely wrapped up with hanging a unit of blood. She chewed on her lower lip, like she used to whenever she'd concentrated on anything.

How had he missed it? All the parts were there, though skewed a bit by time.

Thirteen years had made some major changes to both of them.

Before inserting the catheter, he looked at her one more time. Sure enough, it was January Stewart…the biggest love and the worst heartbreak of his life.

Jan had managed to avoid Beck after the gunshot-wound patient had been prepped and awaited transfer to surgery. She'd passed him off on a younger nurse who was already captivated by his strikingly handsome looks and who gladly agreed to assist him. As long as Gavin didn't find out and he got emergency practice, it would make no difference which nurse assisted Beck.

He didn't react or seem to mind.

Anyhow, there was a group of needy residents with an assortment of patients to keep her busy. And she was.

She'd spent thirteen years putting her life in order. Just because Beck had been her big love in high school it didn't mean they had anything to reminisce about. Their horrible ending tugged at Jan's conscience. But now was not the time to relive the past. It couldn't be changed.

She tamped down the memories and tried not to cringe. Not today. Not when the emergency department was crawling with patients.

Jan escorted her next patient into the last available ER room and handed the young man a gown. "What seems to be the problem?"

"I think I have an infected spider bite, and now it's spreading."

He showed her his thigh. She put on a disposable glove and gently touched a red, raised, angry-looking boil. It was warm and definitely infected.

"How long have you had this?"

"About a week now."

She noticed little pimple-like satellite areas budding around it. "Any fever?"

The patient shook his head no. "But it keeps getting bigger."

Before she could put the digital thermometer into his mouth, a shadow fell on her.

"Looks like MRSA."

She glanced over her shoulder and found Beck. Methecillin-resistant staph aureus was a perplexing condition, cropping up in and out of hospitals. How he could make a snap diagnosis like that astounded her. And blurting it out right in front of the patient showed poor judgement.

"I'll have Dr. Riordan take a look," she said, dismissing Beck.

"You play team sports?" Beck walked around her and faced the patient.

"I'm on a football team."

"Anyone else have 'spider bites'?"

"You know, a couple other guys might, come to think of it. We thought we got 'em on our last away game."

Beck glanced at Jan. "Trust me, its MRSA. If we don't treat it properly now, he runs the risk of developing myositis. Rather than wasting time treating with the wrong antibiotic, I'd lance and drain it, get a culture tonight. Save the cost of an expensive antibiotic and a return visit to the ER."

"We'll be right back." Jan strained a smile at the patient,

excused herself from the bedside and escorted Beck out of the room by his elbow. "What are you doing?" she said, once in the hall. "The kid hasn't even been examined by a doctor yet, and you're already diagnosing and treating him?"

"I've been in the military for years and I've seen MRSA all over the place. Believe me, it's a waste of time treating him with antibiotics alone, especially if the staph infection is resistant to it. He'll just be back in here next week with more of those boils, and they'll be ten times worse."

Jan glared at him, until he gave her a sarcastic smile. She hated it when he grinned so smugly like that. Just like the time standing by the lockers in high school after art class when he'd first figured out how much she'd liked him. She spun around and strode down the hall to Dr. Riordan's office. He'd obviously figured out who she was. Her only line of defense? Avoid him!

"Dr. Riordan, can you do a quick examination of a spider bite?" She glanced down the hall to find Beck already gathering the equipment he'd need to lance and drain the eruption, and her face went angrily hot. She bit back her thoughts and followed Dr. Riordan down to the exam room, hoping he'd put Beck in his place.

After doing a quick assessment and patient interview the doctor said, "Looks like MRSA."

So much for back-up.

"We can either treat you with broad-spectrum antibiotics, which may or may not help, or we can open and drain the area tonight, stitch you up and send you home. We'll get culture results in forty-eight hours and make sure you're on the right antibiotic. Then you can follow up with your primary-care physician next week."

Jan felt conspired against as she chewed her lower lip and had the patient sign the consent for the procedure. She started to leave the room when Beck rolled his tray of equipment inside.

"Stick around," he said. "I'll need your help."

The exam room took on a red cast as she swallowed her anger and nodded her head, knowing this was a one-man job. As long as he didn't let on that he knew who she was, she'd play along with his little game, even if it meant her blood pressure getting elevated.

With her throat growing sorer by the minute, and her nasal congestion getting worse, she'd avoid him tomorrow by calling in sick to work.

Beck finished the last stitch and turned to Jan. "You can take it from here."

She nodded dutifully, but refused to look at him. He smiled at the patient, who thanked him, then left the room.

It was almost more than he could do not to grab her by the arm and drag her down the hall to some secluded place and tell her exactly how she'd screwed up his life. Oh, but he'd had the last laugh because he'd risen above all the dirt everyone in Atwater had tried to dump on him his whole life. He'd proved wrong everyone who'd said he would never amount to anything. He'd served his country well, seen more countries than most people dreamed about, and now he proudly wore the LAPD badge and served on the elite SWAT team. For someone who'd received the infamous honor in his senior class of being tagged "most likely to wind up in a correctional center" he'd done pretty damn well for himself.

Beck straightened his shoulders and swaggered toward the doctors' lounge. He needed a drink, but a good strong cup of coffee would have to do instead.

Jan finally had a chance to take her dinner break around eight p.m. She notified Carmen and headed for the nurses' lounge. Unable to wait one more second to read the special letter, she dug it out of her pocket and ripped it open. This time every year, as promised, the updated letter arrived.

A shining smile from Meghan Jean greeted her inside the envelope. She'd be twelve and a half now, and in seventh grade. Long dark brown French braids rested on her bony shoulders. A handful of freckles were sprinkled across her nose, a nose very much like Jan's. But the eyes were definitely placed and shaped like her father's, except their color was blue…like hers.

Dear January,

We're reporting in on this year's progress with our daughter. Meghan has joined the track team and also loves to dance. She scored in the top ten percent for her annual scholastic testing and her teachers want to place her in some gifted classes. It seems that out of the blue she has discovered a love of art, and wants to take painting classes. She continues to be a warm and loving girl with a natural excitement and curiosity for life even though puberty is fast approaching. Meghan absolutely hates wearing braces, but we've discovered clear wires and sometimes she likes to have bright blue ones applied just for fun. As you know, she's quite the ham and keeps Daryl and me laughing. We promised her a Disney World vacation this year and she can barely go to sleep each night from thinking about it.

On another note, something new has cropped up in school. Meghan's science class is studying genetics and genealogy and she is suddenly bursting with questions about her birth parents. Would it be okay for us to tell her a bit more about you? We understand that you never named the father, but if there is any information whatsoever you can provide, we'd appreciate it.

As always, Daryl and I are so grateful to you for your unselfish act and want you to know we treat our daughter as the precious gift she is. We pray that life is treating you well.

All the best,
The Williams

The last part of the letter went blurry. Had it been an unselfish act? Could giving her daughter away to strangers in an open adoption be considered anything less than an easy way out for a frightened seventeen-year-old? Sure, they had been well screened, willing and anxious to become parents, but they'd solved her "problem" and life had never been the same since.

She glanced again at the school picture, and choked back her tears.

The door flew open behind her. "Apparently only the nurses keep fresh coffee in the pot," Beck said.

Jan startled, dropping the letter, and the picture went

flying through the air to the floor. She scrambled to reach it before Beck could see, but he was just as quick.

She leaned. He knelt. They almost bumped heads. They looked into each other's eyes. Fear of being found out sent a rocket fueled with adrenaline through her chest. His hand rested on top of hers on the picture on the floor.

CHAPTER TWO

"SO HOW'VE you been, *January*?" Beck asked, glancing up from the overturned picture on the floor and staring deep into her eyes.

Jan glanced into Beck's challenging glare and willed herself not to shake. She swallowed a hard lump and narrowed her gaze, then reverted to old, well-practiced techniques of evasion.

"I've been fantastical, Beck. And you?" She gingerly retrieved the photograph of her daughter from the floor and slipped it back inside her pocket before he had a chance to see it.

"Outstanding. I've been outstanding."

Was his point to let her know how well he'd gotten along in life without her? To point out that leaving her behind and joining the army had made him "all that he could be" like the ad on the military poster said? Or was he lying through his teeth, like she was?

He seemed on the verge of saying something more.

Before Jan could begin to decipher the multitude of expressions in his eyes, Carmen appeared in the doorway.

"Here you are. I've got good news," she said, looking

toward Beck. "Gavin has arranged for you to scrub in with the gunshot wound. You'd better high-tail it up there before anyone changes their mind."

"Fantastical," he said, slanting a glance Jan's way. A grim look that promised they hadn't even begun to broach the subject foremost on their minds. Then Beck swept out of the tiny room without looking back, leaving a gust of air that seemed to strangle her instead of offer relief.

Carmen leaned against the door frame, cocking a brow. "Did he just say 'fantastical'?"

Jan nodded solemnly.

"He's kind of cute, don't you think?" Carmen continued.

"I hadn't noticed."

"Then those glasses are the wrong prescription. Did I interrupt something?"

"Not at all. He was just looking for a decent cup of coffee, and, being a smart guy, knew to come to the nurses' lounge." She feigned a carefree smile, gathered her letter and lunch items and hustled back to work.

The next day, her guilty conscience wouldn't let her call in sick to work. Sure, her nose was congested, but she wasn't running a fever and she could sneeze into the crook of her elbow on the job if needed. If her condition warranted it, she'd don a mask. But knowing the glut of emergencies on weekends, not to mention the people without health insurance who used the ED as their doctor's office on their days off, she couldn't leave Carmen short a nurse for a shift.

She'd tried all night long not to recall the challenge in Beck's glare when he'd asked how she'd been. Not answering his calls and letters when he'd shipped out for boot-camp had been the second-hardest thing she'd ever had to do. Even with her heart aching for the boy she'd loved since tenth grade, nothing had compared with the pain of giving up their child for adoption.

That was all in the past now. They were grown-ups with careers and personal commitments. She assumed Beck had responsibilities, being both a medic in the National Guard and on the SWAT team. She could only imagine the different countries he'd been sent to in the last thirteen years, and she'd never even ventured out of California.

She hadn't noticed a wedding ring on his hand when he'd reached for the picture in the nurses' lounge. Why did that somehow garner a feeling of relief?

Jan shook her head, popped a twelve-hour antihista-mine, and dressed for work.

On the drive to Mercy Hospital, she turned on the radio and heard the two o'clock news. There had been a car chase which had turned into a hostage situation and from there escalated into a stand-off in an apartment building in the Wilshire area of Los Angeles. Her mind shot to Beck. Would he be called in with the SWAT team to handle this explosive situation? Anxiety welled up, as if a tight squeez-ing harness was wrapped around her chest, with the knowl-edge he could be in harm's way. But that was the life he'd chosen for himself, and he was no longer her business.

When she arrived at work to an already hopping emergency department, there was no sign of Beck. She pondered the hostage situation and Beck's possible in-volvement. The thought that he was otherwise engaged and that she might not have to face him in the ER that night didn't soothe her mounted concern in the least.

A wild and crazy Saturday night in the emergency department had postponed Jan's meal break until nine p.m. The inundated ER felt stifling and she went outside for fresh air. She found a secluded bench and was unwrapping her sandwich for dinner when the loud rumble of a motorcycle rolling into the parking lot broke the silence. The rider gave one last rev of the engine, parked, and threw his leg over the machine as if he were a wrangler, a helmet in place of a cowboy hat.

The leather jacket and the swagger unmistakably belonged to Beck. Apparently he still preferred motorcycles to cars. What was he doing here? She hadn't had time to catch the news and didn't know whether the earlier incident had been resolved or not but, even so, why would he report to the ED after such an intense afternoon and evening?

A quick flash of the undaunted guy she'd once dated appeared before her. He'd been pegged as a troublemaker since grammar school and had never lived his reputation down. He'd played along and acted the role of bad boy all through high school, but Jan had known the softer, more playful side of him. They'd laughed together just as much as they'd kissed or argued. She'd never understood why he'd let people think so little of him, expecting the worse and assuming when anything had gone wrong that he'd been at the core of it.

They'd met in an open-grade art class when she had been a sophomore and he a junior, and had bonded over painting delicate eggshells. He'd helped her pass algebra and walked her through her science experiments whenever she'd been confused. He'd been the guy to hold her until her tears had dried after her dog got hit by a car. No one else had seemed to see the noble and tender side of Beck but her...back then.

She sighed and suddenly lost her appetite. It had hurt like hell to break up with him all those years ago. And what must he have thought of her for the cowardly way she'd done it?

By the time her meal break was up, Beck had already donned scrubs and was tending to a laceration in one of the emergency exam rooms. She tiptoed by, only to be snagged by Carmen.

"We've got a DUI in transit. The guy wrapped his car around a telephone pole and partially scalped himself. Gavin wants Beck to stitch him up, so get a minor operations kit and meet him in the procedure room pronto."

Jan nodded, wishing they'd assign Beck to someone else, but she needed to accept there'd be no getting away from the ex-love of her life for the next month.

In a world where justice had a way of weaseling its way in at the most inconvenient times, she knew this would be her punishment for lying to him.

Fifteen minutes later Jan cleaned the wound. She flushed the patient's skin with copious amounts of saline followed by antiseptic solution then patted it dry with sterile towels. The majority of the patient's hair was intact. A full head of brown hair had been partially severed from the forehead back, looking like a floppy, cheap toupee. She'd never seen anything like it before outside old cowboy and Indian movies.

Jan dabbed at the last few trickles of blood as Beck

injected a local anesthetic along the forehead and waited for it to take effect. She avoided his eyes as much as possible after his initial raised brow and shake of the head when first examining the wound. But occasionally their gazes met. Each and every time small explosions of adrenaline made her tremble. She prayed he couldn't tell.

Jan had to admit Beck was a skilled clinician. But even with his expert suturing, the patient would have a thin white scar along his hairline for the rest of his life to remind him of his bonehead decision to drive while drunk.

Fortunately, the patient was still inebriated enough not to mind having his scalp sewn back onto his head. Thankful for the mask she'd opted to wear to protect the patient against her cold, she didn't have to breathe in his liquor fumes first hand.

Beck concentrated, using a curved needle in a holder and toothed forceps to help insert the needle through the thick skin and out again. He made even stitches with fine braided silk, taking meticulous care to fit the jigsaw pattern of the "scalping" together. He'd divided the wound into manageable lengths, placing a suture at the halfway and quarter points to avoid "dog-ears"—unequal bites of tissue that would heal with gaps. Even without the help of the plastics department, the patient stood a good shot of healing with minimal visible scarring—as long as his hairline didn't recede.

Once the tedious procedure of what seemed no less than fifty stitches concluded, Beck dropped the needles into the sharps container on the wall and, gathering the remaining instruments, helped Jan clean up.

"I can do this," she said, dismissing his efforts.

"Just trying to help, January." He wadded up the betadine-stained blue paper barrier and tossed it, like a basketball, into the nearby trash can. It landed perfectly, and Beck stared at Jan with deep-set penetrating eyes that almost made her knees buckle.

He'd matured and grown into a formidably handsome man. Muscle had thickened and replaced the lanky limbs of his youth. With his hair nearly completely shaved, his features seemed all the more chiseled and striking. The old trace of a furrowed brow had settled more deeply into the map of his forehead. Lightly etched squint lines hinted at the many sights he'd seen since his departure from her life.

He'd once had thick wavy dark hair and he'd worn it styled and gelled to perfection. He'd warn her not to mess with his do and she'd complain about how he always managed to ruin her hairstyle and then she'd run her fingers through his hair just to spite him. Typical of high-school students, they'd end their silly challenges and arguments by glaring at one another, calling each other a name, and rushing into a smoldering make-up kiss.

He'd changed dramatically, and, if possible, for the better. His sexy appeal sent chills undulating through her body. How would she survive the next month?

Deep in myriad thoughts, she spun round and bumped Beck with the kidney basin filled with antiseptic. Some spilled over the brim, splattering onto his scrub top. He held her wrists to steady her hands and she panicked.

"I told you I don't need your help. This wouldn't have happened if you'd just let things be," she said, clenching her jaw.

He pried her fingers free of the basin, all the while

keeping eye contact, then dipped his gloved fingertips into the solution and flicked it at close range onto her scrub top. Jerk. He strolled to the sink and poured the rest of the liquid down the drain.

"Now we're even, *January*," he said in a familiar taunting whisper. If it were only that simple. He seemed to seethe whenever he looked at her. Could she blame him?

The inebriated patient lay snoozing, oblivious to his surroundings.

The look in Beck's eyes dared her to challenge him. He may have over a decade's worth of questions for her, but she couldn't allow him to become familiar with her again. There was too much at stake. She'd endured the pain alone for years and could think of no good reason to share it with him. He'd only hate her more.

"Call me Jan, please. And I'd appreciate it if you'd keep our past out of this place. No one needs to know about us."

One brow rose slowly and he nodded, the hazel gaze muted by a cautious veil. "Still worried about your reputation, I see," he said, before turning and leaving the room.

The patient snored and Jan wanted to scream. After thirteen years of hiding from her past, doing everything she could to respect her decision instead of loathing herself, it had finally caught up with her. Sheer reflex made her want to run into the night. But she'd prided herself in growing up and facing the toughest parts of her life head on. If spending the next month working with the father of her child—the baby she'd given up for adoption—was the price she would have to pay, she'd pay it. And at the end she'd try to do what she'd done for years—forget and move on.

* * *

Beck had seen men die before his eyes. He'd lived by his wits and survived close call after close call in battles across the globe. He'd defied his parents, who'd always thought he was too hard to handle, he'd proved his high-school principal wrong with his predictions of incarceration. Now Beck was one of the "good" guys. And where had it gotten him?

Hell, he'd given up the one person he'd ever loved for the sake of his quest for adventure. Breaking free of Atwater had meant that much to him. Nothing, he'd sworn, would hold him back from grabbing life by the tail and holding on for a wild ride. Except the "wild ride" had included pain and suffering and memories he wished to God he could get out of his head.

After all of that, how could the simple task of brushing up his medic skills throw him for such a loop?

Beck knew the reason. The task involved being near the one person who'd taught him the purest and most honest feeling he could ever hope to experience. Love. Of course, she'd been the one to rip that same feeling out of his chest and ruin it for the rest of his life. No other woman had ever gotten to know that vulnerable secret part of his soul since January Stewart. It had ruined more than his share of otherwise satisfying relationships, too.

January had ripped away any chance of trusting a woman that much again when she'd refused to wait for him. When she'd coldly broken off their relationship over the phone, and only then after he'd tried to track her down through some friends. At first he'd thought she was paying him back for leaving her and joining the army, but her decision to break up with him had gone beyond stubborn resolve or hurt. He'd never been able to pinpoint what the missing piece of the puzzle was, but in his gut he knew there was something more to their break-up. He'd given up guessing what long ago.

Beck shook his head. The new version of his first love stood right inside the Mercy Hospital emergency ward and the thought made his blood boil. She'd screwed him up beyond all recognition when she'd dumped him. He'd spent three months dreaming about her in bootcamp. Sometimes the hell he'd had to endure in training had only been bearable because of her face smiling at him in his mind. Her soft lips had teased him, "Don't be a wuss. You can do it." The flood of memories that her presence had released just now in the exam room was almost more than he could bear. Good thing he had been wearing gloves when he held her wrists. He wasn't sure how he'd have reacted if they'd been skin to skin.

He shook his head and smiled ruefully. He didn't care that she still affected him. It didn't matter that whatever it was that had once appealed to him hadn't faded. Her allure had only grown stronger. He wouldn't fall for it. Never again. He'd never forgive or trust her again.

A familiar phrase his drill sergeant had repeated over and over popped into his brain, "Don't get mad. Get even."

Hmm. Was revenge as sweet as everyone stacked it up to be?

Beck looked up from his thoughts in time to see Gavin Riordan approaching. "Hey, great job tonight."

"Thanks."

"So what happened with that car chase today?"

"It's a long story," Beck said, scratching the back of his neck.

"The shift's over. Why don't you let me buy you a drink and you can tell me about it?"

Gavin was bending over backwards to help Beck avoid losing time off the job by flying back to North Carolina for his medic update. How could he refuse his request? And after his recent encounter with January, he could definitely use a drink.

"Sure thing. Where're we going?"

"The Emergency Room."

Jan folded her OR gown and pushed it into the dirty clothes hamper. She sat on the bench and untied her shoelaces as Carmen entered the nurses' locker room.

"Hey, Jan. After all this nonstop action tonight, I'm having a hard time unwinding. You want to get a drink with me?"

"Nah. I'm coming down with a cold."

Carmen rarely asked Jan to do anything close to socializing. She felt kind of bad, refusing her.

"A hot toddy might be just what the doctor ordered. You know what I mean?" Carmen added.

Jan dragged in an indecisive breath.

Looking disappointed, Carmen said, "Well, if you change your mind, I'll be in the Emergency Room."

The Emergency Room was the after-hours hang out for many of the Mercy Hospital staff. She knew exactly where it was, though rarely went there.

Deciding that Carmen probably had something on her mind and needed a friendly ear, Jan reconsidered. The fact that she was dreading another night of tossing and turning with visions of Beck Braxton in her head helped change her mind.

"You know, a hot toddy might just be the ticket. Give me a second to change out of my scrubs and I'll meet you."

"Why don't we drive over together?" Carmen shoved her arm into a black jacket. "I'll drop you back at the parking lot on our way home."

Jan shimmied out of her scrubs. "You're on, but just one drink."

"Sure, just like the doctor ordered," Carmen said, as she left the locker room, leaving the door to flap behind her.

Similar to a real emergency room, the bar was busy and noisy, but that was where the similarities ended. Dark and fueled with a completely different kind of energy, the tables and booths were close to overflowing that Saturday night. The latest female *American Idol* winner belted out a song through the piped-in music. A heated game of darts went on in a corner called the "Surgical Ward" and the adjacent billiards room had a sign over the door, "Hospital Administration."

Carmen pointed out an empty booth, grabbed January's hand and led her to the back of the room. While passing the bar she ordered their drinks and showed the bartender where they were headed.

No sooner had they sat down than Gavin Riordan appeared.

"What's he doing here?" Jan blurted.

"Beth took the twins to visit their grandmother in Florida. And his son's away on a Scouting trip for the weekend. He must be lonely."

Jan smiled at the newly domesticated head of ER. She would never have believed a quiet allergy nurse could have tamed her boss when she'd first started working at the Mercy Hospital ER two years ago. It only went to show that miracles could happen.

Carmen waved him over.

"Ladies." Gavin nodded and pushed his way into the booth next to Carmen. "The drinks are on me."

"That's fine with me, as long as they aren't going to deduct this from my Christmas bonus." Carmen sprang into action with her boss. Sure, they spent most of their time at work verbally sparring, but no one was fooled by their antics. They'd go to the mat for each other in a heartbeat.

"You didn't get the memo about the suspension of all bonuses this year?" he chided.

"Don't even go there," Carmen snarled.

The drinks arrived and Gavin paid.

"Bring a couple of beers, OK?" he instructed the waitress.

"You drinking for two tonight?" Carmen asked, with a mock-innocent toss of her head.

Before Gavin had a chance to answer, Jan's heart dropped. Pushing through the crowd was the unmistakable figure of Atwater's notorious bad boy, Beck Braxton. What was she supposed to do now?

She cast a terrified glance around the bar for an emergency exit. "Listen, I've got to go." Jan started to stand, but Gavin's strong grasp kept her from reaching her full height.

"Have a seat," he said. "You're among friends."

He had no idea the fire he was playing with. In panic mode, Jan darted her gaze to Carmen.

"Drink your toddy and relax. That guy's a hunk by anyone's standards. I should be so lucky." Carmen took a deep swig of her white wine and gave a Cheshire-cat smile that Jan had an overwhelming desire to scratch off her face. Relax? Easy for her to say.

Beck's step faltered when Jan peered out of the booth and caught his gaze. He recovered so quickly, anyone with less of a trained eye would never have noticed. She did what she'd been told and gulped the warm brandy-and-honey concoction and tried to act nonchalant when he reached their table.

Beck filled the only remaining spot in the booth, the seat beside her.

"I ordered you a beer," Gavin piped up.

Beck nodded his thanks and glanced to his side, at Jan. She wondered if her smile looked as unconvincing as his. They all sat in momentary silence and sipped their respective drinks. Gavin broke the silence with a question for Beck.

The men discussed the day's events, and Carmen sat rapt, chin in palm, swigging her wine and listening. With the aid of the twelve-hour antihistamine, Jan's drink swirled through her head and soon she found it hard to focus. Dull buzzing droned in her ears. Occasionally Carmen would kick her foot under the table to urge her to join the conversation. Jan ignored her and sat mute, staring at her hands.

Soon a warm blush settled in and she loosened the top button of her shirt to help cool off. She hadn't felt this uncomfortable since the first day of open-grade art class when she had been fifteen, and seventeen-year-old Beck had been her big secret crush and had taken a seat next to her.

Jan blinked and squinted to try and focus better. As far as men went, Beck was an incredible specimen. Dappled shadows from the bar lights accentuated the line of his jaw and the depth of his eyes. Still, his magnetism frightened her. She didn't dare study him for long.

"Are you OK?" Beck asked, bumping her thigh with his knee under the table.

"I'm feeling a little strange. What'd they put in this drink?" She turned to Carmen.

"Brandy. When's the last time you had a real drink?" Carmen tossed her a disbelieving glance.

"I've *never* had brandy."

Carmen raised her hands and glared at her boss. "Guys, I swear I had no idea the woman was so backward."

Gavin chuckled and finished his beer. "You need a ride home, Jan?"

"Carmen's going to drop me back at my car."

Beck broke in. "You shouldn't be driving. I'll take you home."

Jan glanced toward Carmen for help. She found evasive eyes and a fidgety hand smoothing coarse black hair. Wasn't she going to bail her out? Knowing Beck, he'd grill her until she'd told him the truth about why she'd broken up with him. She wasn't anywhere ready to tell him what had happened. What in the world should she do now?

Beck stood at the exact moment Gavin did. They shook hands goodnight, and Carmen skirted behind them and headed for the door.

"Thanks a million," Jan said under her breath, leaning out of the booth.

"I should be so lucky," Carmen whispered, tossing a glance Beck's way. Jan stood along with everyone else. Soon she'd be on her own...with her ex.

She weaved fingers through her short bob and straightened her glasses. The drink may have soothed her throat, but she felt wobbly, parched and edgy. Realizing Beck was checking out her low-slung second-skin jeans, she quickly put on her extra-long sweater. His eyes traveled back to her face.

"You can wear my helmet."

Her head shot up the moment she realized the mode of travel Beck had in mind.

"It's against California law to ride without a helmet."

"I'll have to take that chance, won't I?" Typical of Beck. "You look like you need some water," he said.

She sat back down on the booth bench. "A cup of tea might help clear my head."

Beck raised his hand and flagged down the waitress. "A tea and some water, please."

"Then let me get a cab," Jan said.

He shook his head. "That would be too convenient." His irritated stare let her know in no uncertain terms he was no happier about this than she was. So why had he offered? "I think you're overdue for a ride on my chopper." A punishing smile thinned his lips.

Jan found it hard to sip tea through a locked jaw, especially with Beck sitting across from her, glaring.

"What?" she challenged.

"What do you mean, what?" He played dumb, but never broke his stare.

"We both know you've got an axe to grind with me."

He crossed a foot on his knee and continued to bore a hole into her head with his stare. "So true."

She defied him, refusing to look away, and drank more tea, though it burned all the way down. His long fingers tapped rhythmically on the tabletop. She took another punishing sip. He cleared his throat.

"You know, it's customary when people say they love each other to keep in touch when one goes away."

"I didn't realize you were such a traditionalist, Beck. I thought you couldn't get out of Atwater fast enough."

It hurt like hell to be flippant, but she had no choice tonight. Now wasn't the time or place to sort out their differences. She'd made her choice years ago and he couldn't find out about her secret. Not tonight. Not ever. Not if she could help it.

"We had an agreement, January."

"Too bad, so sad, guess I broke it."

Beck went completely still. Warning cold serpent eyes sent a chill slithering down her spine. "That's garbage and you know it. Level with me. Your mother sent you away, didn't she?"

She vehemently shook her head. "Nope. I wanted to go."

"Where? Where did you go?"

"To modeling school."

"Then why are you a nurse?"

"Look at me, Beck. Do I look like model material to you?"

At a stalemate, they stared at each other across the booth, the dim lights hiding the truth.

"Let's go," he said, standing to his full six feet two inches.

Jan would rather have walked home barefoot on hot coals than ride on the back of his Harley. What had once been exhilarating and sexy as all hell had suddenly turned into an exercise in torture.

CHAPTER THREE

DETERMINED not to make physical contact with Beck on the motorcycle, Jan pushed as far back on the pillion as it allowed. She planted her feet on the bars and braced her hands behind her along the edge of the elongated seat, gritting her teeth as if doing so would keep her steady and safe. Once settled, she gave Beck directions to her house.

She used to love riding on the back of Beck's motorbike, but this time it made her feel jittery and tightly strung. Out of practice, she stared at the back of his neck rather than watch the road spin by.

The moonlit sky and pleasant temperature normally would have made for a perfect night to ride with the top down in a car. But this? Completely vulnerable on the back of Beck's bike, she chewed on her lower lip and prayed she'd make it home in one piece. When had she become such a chicken?

After a stoplight, he jumped into what felt like hyper-speed and her hands went flying around his leather-covered torso. But Beck was on a residential street where the speed limit was thirty-five m.p.h. What felt like reckless abandon to Jan was probably because of the hot toddy and the real speed doubtless closer to twenty-five.

Turning her face, if it weren't for the bulky helmet, she'd have smashed her cheek against his back. He stiffened and sat a bit straighter. As it was, her chin dug into the muscle just above his scapula. Solid and steady, he stayed ramrod straight, making it easier for her to anchor herself to him.

A quick reminder of the stable force he'd once been should have helped her relax. It didn't. Her arms were around the last man on earth she'd ever wanted to see again.

Jan clenched her eyes tight and held on as if her life depended on it, and remained that way for several minutes until he slowed down and entered her driveway.

What would her neighbors think about the quiet and withdrawn condo dweller arriving home well after midnight on the back of a chopper? It almost made her grin, but she remembered who the driver was, and lost all sense of amusement.

After forcing her eyes open, she jumped off the bike before he had a chance to help. She almost lost her balance but managed to steady herself after a series of klutzy hops. Rather than watch his long legs and tight ass when he expertly removed himself from the machine, she fidgeted with the helmet. Yeah, she'd peeked first. Her hands fluttered and made little progress in loosening the strap.

"Here," he said, stepping too close and reaching for her. "Let me get that."

Like magic he unlatched it and had her free and clear in a flash. She swallowed and stepped back quickly, almost tripping on the curb. He caught her by the elbow.

"Whoa. You OK?"

"I'm fine. Fine. Thanks for the ride. Goodnight." She

wanted to run but decided it would be too obvious. Avoiding his eyes, she turned and forced a normal pace toward her porch. He strode right behind.

"I'm fine, remember? You don't have to see me to my door."

"What would your mother think if I didn't?"

Her mother? When had been the last time she had considered what her mother thought about anything? Ever since Karen Stewart had told her to "get rid of it", as if Jan's pregnancy had been nothing more than an inconvenience, she'd questioned her mother's advice on anything.

Beck used to go out of his way to impress Mrs. Stewart, as if knowing that the key to any girl's heart started by winning over the mother. Karen had been anything but impressed with the wild and edgy teen, and Jan had never been able to convince her otherwise. His joining the Army and her subsequent pregnancy news had had Karen cursing Beck's very existence. It seemed she'd had plans of pushing her daughter into the limelight, with high hopes of making a buck or two off her looks. The pregnancy had forced Karen to come up with a different idea. She'd refused the traditional adoption agency the school counselor had found, instead finding an ad in a local paper and pursuing private, open adoption with a couple and a special lawyer willing to pay more than the usual prenatal health-care fees. Then she'd forced her underage daughter to lie.

Jan and Beck reached her door and she fished through her purse for the key. Once she found it, she glanced up. Beck was staring at her with intent dark eyes. Sharp angles of moonlight and porch lamp shadowed the serious mask of his face. She tried to read his expression but fell short. Something told her to be still.

He moved forward to frame her face with surprisingly warm hands for someone who'd just driven a motorcycle. Cold fear swept over Jan when she realized he planned to kiss her. She sucked in a breath of protest, but was forced to hold it when his lips covered hers. Her hands flapped at her sides. His hungry, searching kiss tore at her good sense. She dropped her purse. Her hands found their way up his arms to his neck, the neck she'd stared at the entire drive home, and she kissed him back.

With mind battling body, her will lost when she parted her lips and stole a taste of Beck's velvet-smooth mouth. His tongue pressed against hers and jagged, raw energy sliced through her center.

Beck.

She remembered his kisses. They always led to heaven…or the back seat of his father's car.

Her lips searched his mouth, drawing on long-forgotten memories of frantic make-out sessions with the hottest boy in high school. The guy all of her friends had warned her against getting involved with. The one who'd taken her virginity on a special night she'd never forget as long as she lived.

The father of the baby she'd lied about. The baby she had given away.

Beck.

His demanding kiss guided her from far-away thoughts back to the moment. The man still had it, and she felt whatever "it" was all the way down to her toes. With her body swirling with sensations, and her knees growing weaker by the second, she somehow managed to come to her senses and tore away from the dangerous kiss.

She shook her head and sputtered for air. "What the hell are you trying to do?"

Calculating hazel eyes delved deep beyond her guard. "Just testing," he said.

She shuddered.

He bent down and picked up her purse, handing it to her. "Goodnight, January," he said, as if he hadn't felt a thing. "I'll see you at the hospital."

Stunned, she watched Beck saunter to his motorcycle, put on the helmet, rev the engine and ride off into the night. By the time he'd disappeared round the corner, her heart still hadn't figured out what a normal rhythm was.

What the hell had he been thinking? Beck hit the freeway at breakneck speed. Maybe he could ride off the old feeling that had penetrated the barrier around his heart. Damn! It was supposed to have been a revenge kiss, angry and rude, but it had quickly turned into a steam-up-January's-glasses-and-mess-with-Beck's-head kind of kiss. Wearing the heavy armor of retribution, he hadn't expected to react so thoroughly to her. He'd assumed he'd become immune, but time and pain hadn't changed a thing.

The soft, sexy sparks had started almost immediately at the touch of her lips to his, and had soon escalated to near fireworks. Her tongue had nearly driven him out of his mind. It had been all he could do to keep from pressing her against the door and feeling every inch of her. If she hadn't stopped him, he'd be thinking of ways to get inside her house and into her bed right this minute.

This wasn't how he was supposed to get even. He wasn't supposed to want her. If he wanted to get even, he'd have to toughen up, regain her trust, then move in for the payback.

He stepped on the gas and hit the highway as if in a race to save his life.

"Tell me. Tell me. Come on, share." Carmen zipped up beside Jan the moment she arrived at work the next afternoon, already hot and annoyed from the inconvenient bus ride in.

Jan stared straight ahead and kept walking, foolishly hoping to put Carmen off. No such luck.

"You ride off into the night on a Harley with a hunk, and don't have anything to report? You're more messed up than I thought."

"Knock it off. It was just a ride home. You deserted me, and I was stuck with Beck. That's all."

Carmen stopped, arms akimbo. She let out an exasperated sigh. "What flaw did you find this time?"

Jan nailed her with a glare. "He rides a chopper."

Carmen rolled her eyes. "Oh, great. So here we go with another lame excuse from the queen of brush-offs. What was wrong with the last guy you went out with? Oh, yeah, his teeth were too white." She shook her head in a slow, wide swing.

"That guy's teeth were practically fluorescent, Carmen. I couldn't look him in the face without needing sunglasses."

Carmen worked to conceal the crack of a smile. She moved closer and lowered her voice. "Beck is different. You've got to admit, he's a real find. A keeper," she sang. "Why not give him a chance?"

Jan drew a deep breath and adjusted her glasses. "Look. I admit he's a hunk, but let's face it. He's out of my league." She gave a pleading puppy-dog glance. "You don't want to be responsible for my broken heart, do you?"

Carmen slumped her shoulders. "You're impossible. Someday you're going to realize what you've missed out on and regret it." Carmen couldn't possibly know what a home run she'd hit with that bit of wisdom. She raised her hands in defeat. "OK. I give up. I'll butt out."

Knowing Carmen as she did, Jan knew the woman had no intention of butting out. At least Jan had bought herself some time to figure out a strategy of her own on how to deal with the Beck situation.

She spun around and headed toward the triage station. Thankfully tonight it was her turn to assess patients and assign their priority in order of their illness's severity instead of at what time they showed up at the ER. If she played things right, she could possibly avoid Beck the entire shift.

Before she reached her station, Beck appeared at the front desk. Her heart rocked with an unwanted reaction. He looked clean-shaven, and if it were possible, his hair was even shorter. He wore his dark police uniform like a new-age knight, a tall, broad-shouldered, noble public servant. To protect and serve.

Not fair.

When he noticed Jan and quickly looked away, she almost wished things could be normal between them instead of strained. Then she made a beeline for the triage door.

Patients arrived in clumps. Eight different maladies rushed the front desk within five minutes of each other, and Jan worked her way through the problems in order of severity.

The chest pain first, the child with the asthma attack next, the skateboard accident with a potential fracture third. The frequent-flyer migraine and the infected lip piercing would have to wait a bit longer. The rectal pain, "microscopic bugs under the skin," and the new-onset fever and cough would most likely have a two- to three-hour wait before seeing an emergency doctor tonight.

Three hours into the busy Sunday evening shift, a car sped into the red zone directly in front of the emergency entrance. A skinny teenage boy frantically rushed inside.

"I need help," he called to the desk clerk. "My girlfriend just had a seizure."

Jan heard him and rushed to the wheelchair storage area, thankful their stock hadn't been depleted, grabbed one and wheeled it to the curb. A lethargic redhaired girl drowsily lifted her head from the front seat of the car.

"You're going to be OK. You're at the hospital now," Jan reassured her as she assisted the doe-eyed, freckle-faced girl into the wheelchair.

"What happened?" Jan asked as they re-entered the hospital.

The boy jumped in. "We were, like, just talking, and she got this strange look on her face and then, dude, she started shaking. She even foamed at the mouth."

Sluggish, but coming round, the girl was able to give her name, Cassie, and answer the question of where she thought she was. She was a bit foggy on what time it was. While Jan settled her, she asked more questions. Cassie knew the day's date and her birthday. She was only sixteen. Her parents would need to be contacted as her condition wasn't life-threatening.

"Have you had any physical trauma lately? A fall? Bump your head?"

Cassie shook her head. Her vital signs, including her temperature, were normal, with the exception of a rapid heartbeat.

"Take any drugs recently?"

The boyfriend stepped back and got quiet.

"No," Cassie stated.

"Any alcohol today?"

Again she shook her head. Jan hadn't smelled anything obvious either.

"Been sick lately? Have you been getting enough sleep?"

"No and yeah."

"Show how many fingers I'm holding up."

The girl mimicked three digits. A quick head and face exam proved to be normal. A tap test of reflexes in all four extremities was also unremarkable.

"Tell me what happened."

"I dunno. I, like, had this weird feeling and then I was like…here."

"We'll admit you to the emergency ward for a thorough neurological examination, but your parents need to consent before we can do anything."

The attending boy's eyebrows rose and he edged closer to the triage room door.

Cassie lazily nodded her head. "OK," she said.

Jan didn't want to risk putting Cassie back in the waiting room where she'd go unobserved, so she called the ED ward clerk and secured a bed. She also initiated standard protocol orders for the patient—monitor, IV and oxygen—prior to being examined by a doctor.

Jan wheeled Cassie to the ER entry, tapped in the code and waited for the doors to open.

"Look," the boy said, with a skittish glance. "I gotta go. Cass, I'll call you later, OK?"

For the first time during her ER visit Cassie looked alert. "Why?"

"I just gotta. Your parents are coming and all, so that's cool. Look. I'll call ya. *OK?*" He squeezed her shoulder and took off.

Cassie got sullen and slumped in the wheelchair. "Whatever," she said under her breath.

As Jan rolled the girl past the doctor and nurses' station, Carmen indicated room five was vacant. Jan nodded and proceeded toward the room, but on her way made a stop at the linen cart for a few extra bath blankets.

When they arrived in the room, she handed Cassie a hospital gown and pulled the curtain for privacy. The tall teen turned her back to Jan and removed baggy jeans and a loose shirt. Jan padded the bedside rails with the extra blankets as part of the seizure protocol for patient safety. When Cassie had changed, she assisted her into the bed, applied oxygen, blood pressure and oxygen sat monitor and secured the bedrail.

"Was that guy your boyfriend?" Jan asked casually, pretending to be busy with putting the girl's belongings into a large plastic ER patient bag.

Cassie harrumphed. "Used to be." She folded her arms across her chest and stared at the ceiling.

Before starting an IV, Jan placed the personal items bag under the gurney. About to ask if Cassie was sexually active, she noticed the bed shaking. She glanced up to find Cassie rigid, staring at the ceiling with her jaw locked and hands fisted, her legs stiff and straight. The tonic phase of a seizure.

"I need help in room five," she called out, not leaving the bedside.

Cassie had moved into the clonic phase with rhythmic jerky movements when Beck appeared.

"Help me get her on her side so she doesn't aspirate anything."

Beck jumped into action, protecting the girl's head while assisting Jan in turning Cassie onto her side. The patient went back into the stiff tonic phase. Jan turned on the wall suction and hooked up a suction device. She knew not to put anything into a patient's mouth during a seizure, but waited for a chance to suction the excess saliva from the corner of Cassie's mouth.

"How's her O2 sat?" Jan asked, distracted with the convulsing patient.

"It's good," he said, with his large hand guarding Cassie's head as it jerked and twisted.

Having Beck near felt reassuring, though there was nothing they could do until the seizure had settled down. Within another minute Cassie stopped jerking and grinding her teeth. Her heart rate was still rapid, but her blood pressure was normal as was her oxygen level. She stared blankly into the distance.

Jan suctioned her mouth thoroughly, which got a reaction from Cassie. She pulled in her chin and looked annoyed but didn't utter a sound. Beck started an IV in her arm.

Gavin appeared and began issuing orders. "Get a glucose, BUN, 'lytes, drug screen. IV normal saline, TKO. Order a stat EEG and CT scan of the head."

"Write the orders down," Carmen called out from her nurses' station perch. "They're a little busy to take verbal orders, Dr. Riordan." She'd emphasized the word "doctor".

He followed her recommendation, grabbed a green sheet and scribbled out his orders at the nearby patient bedside table.

Beck found the proper-colored tops for the lab-test vials in the IV tray and drew the required blood before hooking up the intravenous line to fluids. Jan noticed the ease with which he worked as she labeled the specimens. She rushed the vials down to the lab to expedite the results and to get away from Beck. After last night's kiss, she couldn't afford to be in the same vicinity as him for any length of time. She couldn't allow herself to fall under his spell and forget the secret that was bound to keep them apart forever.

Jan returned to the triage room, surprised to see the patients with the rectal pain and infected lip piercing still waiting to be seen. The waiting room had filled up again, and a new case needed her immediate attention. Evidently, Sunday night pot roast dinner had turned scary when the forty-six-year-old patriarch had forgotten to chew.

The wife frantically explained they'd tried the Heimlich maneuver, to no avail.

"If he's breathing, there's no need to use that maneuver. See the constant drooling?"

The woman nodded.

"The meat is lodged in his esophagus and he can't swallow it. Fortunately, it's not blocking his airway."

"What does that mean?"

"It means we'll have to call the on-call GI guy to come down and do an endoscopy to remove it."

"Will he be OK?"

"They'll sedate him first, and he should be fine, but he may need to stay overnight for further evaluation."

The drooling man bobbed his head up and down in agreement, looking as though he'd do anything to get the lodged chunk of meat out of his throat.

An hour before the end of shift there was a lull in triage and Jan snuck back to the nurses' lounge for a bottle of water. Gavin called out her name before she could return to her station. He motioned to her from his office to come over.

When she stepped inside, she found Beck already seated. When Dr. Riordan gestured for her to sit, she had no choice but to take the only remaining chair in the room...next to Beck.

"Tell me about Cassie," Gavin started.

Jan leaned forward and took a breath to gather her thoughts. She'd seen so many cases that night she needed to make sure she was talking about the same patient. "The seizure patient?"

"Yeah. It wasn't a seizure."

"What do you mean?" Jan glanced at Beck for back-up.

"You could have fooled me," Beck said.

"The electroencephalograph was normal. Completely normal. So was all of the lab work. The preliminary toxicology is negative for the usual suspects. No cocaine, speed, alcohol, or barbiturates."

They all sat in silence, considering the implications of the findings.

"What about the CT?" Beck asked.

"Normal. No sign of brain lesion or injury."

"Are you saying hers was a pseudo-seizure?" Jan asked.

Gavin shrugged. "Could be."

"Once this soldier in my squad developed seizures and they eventually figured out they were psychogenic in nature," Beck said. "They looked like regular convulsions and he wasn't faking them. They were real to him, but he didn't have any abnormal brainwave activity. Turned out he'd developed post-traumatic stress syndrome and certain sounds and smells triggered these events."

"Cassie mentioned that the boy who brought her in had wanted to break things off today. She didn't seem too upset about it. He couldn't seem to get away fast enough when he heard her parents were coming in, though. I'd never in a million years have guessed that she was faking it."

"She wasn't necessarily faking it. In some instances personal problems can trigger seizure activity, though, like Beck said, it's psychosocial in nature," Gavin said. "I'm admitting her for observation and calling Psych and Neuro in for an evaluation and we'll go from there. But what I do know is, she's pregnant."

Jan's head shot up. "But she's as thin as a waif."

"I know. I stopped the lorazepam the minute I got the results. She may not have told her parents yet, so I'll wait until she's alone and more alert before I talk to her. Anyway, if you guys didn't spot anything else while you were with her, I'd better get on," he said, before bustling off.

Jan glanced at Beck and quickly away, before he could beat her to it. If convulsions could develop from hoarding personal and emotional trauma, or from being unwed and pregnant, hell, she should have been seizing for years now. She shook her head and rose to leave. Beck followed her outside.

He tapped her on the shoulder. She turned and found an earnest expression on his face. "I happened to hear you have tomorrow off, and was wondering if you'd meet me for breakfast."

After a short burst of palpitations, Jan squinted and flashed a glare at Carmen, who averted her eyes rapidly. What should she do? The man should hate her for jilting him all those years ago, yet he'd been a perfect gentleman at work and had just asked her out for an innocent breakfast. Could she trust the amiable smile?

Deep groves bracketed his mouth and stretched all the way down to his chin. His eyes softened with the gesture and she fought the desire to look at him again, more thoroughly.

"Why?" she asked, staring at her feet.

He lowered his voice. "We used to be friends, January. Remember? I'd just like to do some catching up." He lifted his palms. "But if that's not OK with you, I'll understand."

Jan swallowed, guilt rolling in like a huge wave. "I guess breakfast would be OK."

His relieved smile reminded her how easy it had been to fall for him. She couldn't let that ever happen again.

What was his story? Why would he want to spend time with her after she'd done such a dirty trick by running away and breaking things off when he'd needed her most? When she'd needed him most?

Could she trust him with his little innocent breakfast proposal, or was she walking into some kind of trap?

CHAPTER FOUR

THE next morning, not wanting to wear anything suggestive, Jan dressed carefully in a red Mexican-styled blouse with a bright embroidered bib for her breakfast date with Beck. He'd suggested the Pancake House, and she couldn't help but think he'd chosen their favorite teenage haunt in Glendale as a reminder. Amazingly, the place hadn't changed much at all.

Jan entered the A-frame building to find Beck already seated in a booth near the entrance. She wrapped the sweater she'd thrown over her shoulders tighter and tied the sleeves around her neck. The old lime green vinyl seats may have been replaced with plusher patterned wine-colored upholstery, but she'd quickly realized he'd chosen their favorite booth, the one by the full-length triangular window. She'd be extra-careful not to get drawn in with nostalgia.

With unreadable eyes, Beck watched her approach and stood when she got closer. "Good morning," he said with a nod.

"Hi." She glanced around. "It's amazing this place is still in business."

He handed her a large menu. "They've even upgraded the food with a few 'lite' and healthy items."

The mundane conversation helped her slip into her seat and deal with the unavoidable anxiety that welled up inside. Meeting Beck for a meal for the first time in thirteen years took more courage than she'd ever dreamed. She tried to ignore the tingling in her palms and twitchy over-sensitive feel of her skin. Recalling the kiss they'd shared on Saturday night, and her rapturous response, she'd do anything to avoid touching him again.

Beck tilted his head. "You look like you're facing a death sentence. That's a little harsh on a guy's ego."

She shook her head, releasing tensed facial muscles. The truth was she didn't think she'd be able to eat a bite around him. "I just haven't had my morning coffee yet, that's all."

He studied her face, and she knew he didn't buy one phony word she'd uttered. He waved for the waitress. "Two coffees, please."

Jan drew a deep breath to force herself to relax, but the tactic failed miserably. Her hands twined into a ball on the table. Why in the world had she consented to meet him?

"So what's it going to be, a short stack?" he asked with a mischievous glint in his gaze soon after the waitress had left the table.

Why did she allow herself to look into his eyes? There was no trace left of the determined boy she'd once loved. He was all man, confident and proud. She, on the other hand, had all of a sudden reverted to the shy and uncertain tenth-grader on their first date. No. She couldn't think of this as a date. It was strictly a get-together to touch base and "check in" with an old friend after a long absence.

"A short stack sounds good," she said.

"That's more like it."

"The pancakes?"

"The blouse. It looks more like the girl I remember. All bright colors and attitude."

Her cheeks warmed and she reached for the glass of ice water. That girl had been missing since her pregnancy. "I wasn't nearly as flashy as you paint me."

"You were flashy, January. Trust me." He gave a knowing grin, approval written all over his face. "That's part of what I dug about you."

She shook her head, a hot blush rising from her neck. Flashy or not, she had trusted him, with all of her heart, but look where that had gotten her.

"Level with me—whatever happened to the modeling career?" he continued.

Did he have to remember everything? "That was my mother's idea," she bluffed, and hoped he didn't catch on.

"I'll say. She went out of her way to send you to some special school during your senior year. Isn't that what you said when you finally called me? Why didn't you pursue it?"

The "school" had all been part of the story her mother had helped her fabricate to avoid telling her friends, and especially Beck, that she'd been pregnant. "Truth was, the modeling was my mother's dream, not mine. She was a teenage mother and single parent. She felt her dreams got stomped on before they ever hatched. We actually don't talk much any more now that she's married."

"She got married?"

Jan nodded. "Some guy from Vegas. I see her maybe twice a year." If he wanted to put her on the spot, she could do a little delving, too. "So, tell me, Beck, why haven't you married and settled down?"

One brow subtly lifted. "OK, let's change the subject." He stretched his shoulders and reached for his ice water. "Police work has one of the highest divorce rates of any job. I've been obligated to the National Guard for the last ten years, and if I want to collect a decent pension from them someday I'll have to sign on for another ten. But the truth is I'm lousy at relationships." He looked sheepishly at her. "I guess you already know that." He gave a distracted smile as the waitress arrived with their coffee. "She'll need cream," he directed, without conferring with Jan.

He hadn't forgotten a thing. His voice had grown deeper over the years and the low resonant sound admittedly soothed her jittery nerves. Everything had already happened between them, and as long as she kept the big secret, things couldn't possibly get any worse. Why not relax and enjoy the company of the handsome man sitting across the table?

After she'd ordered pancakes, Jan sipped her coffee and gazed at Beck, who was charming the middle-aged waitress with his soulful eyes and slow drawl. Time spent in the military in the southern U.S. had affected his speech more than he probably realized. The effect was a deadly combination of boyish charisma and in-your-face sex appeal. She disguised a sigh as a mini-yawn and forced her gaze toward the tall fake plant in the corner, doing anything to keep from succumbing to his natural appeal.

After the waitress left, he placed his palms flat on the table and asked, "Since you brought the subject up, why didn't you *stay* married?"

Jan tossed Beck a puzzled glance. "How do you know about my marriage?"

She didn't dare tell him the truth—that she'd married an older man for companionship and that she had never really loved him as a wife should, and when he'd pressed her about having children, she hadn't been able to go through with it. She wouldn't admit to Beck how her heart had turned to stone in order to survive the day she'd lost him.

"Uh, I guess I just assumed it since your name badge says Ashworth instead of Stewart."

"Oh. Right. Well, it was a big mistake. We worked together at another hospital and were great friends and we thought we could make a go of it, so we got married five years ago. Let's just say, after a year we divorced amicably…" They'd filed with irreconcilable differences: he'd loved her but she couldn't love him. Thanks to no-fault divorces in California, the process had been civilized and unemotional. At least for her. The divorce was more proof that she was meant to be alone.

"Sounds as if we're more alike than we thought." He held her gaze. "No kids?"

Her eyes darted from his face to her folded hands. Did he know about Meghan or was he asking about her ex-husband? How could she be a parent to another child after abandoning the first? Her insecurities and guilt had made it impossible for their marriage to survive.

A wave of panic soured the coffee she'd just swallowed. She couldn't tell whether he knew anything or not. "No. We didn't have kids." She avoided Beck's eyes, opting instead to clarify the situation with her ex-husband and sidestep the topic that struck horror in her heart.

She'd lied and given up a baby that Beck had a right to know about. But her mother had threatened to press statutory rape charges against him if Jan didn't do exactly what she'd said. She had only been sixteen at the time she'd become pregnant and seventeen when she delivered, and Karen had had specific plans on how to handle the situation. Looking back, Jan realized she'd had no choice other than refusing to "get rid of it", but to this day she wished things could have been handled differently.

Things grew quiet, on the verge of awkward, when the waitress saved the day by arriving with their breakfast. They both dug in.

After a few minutes Beck broke the silence. "What do you think's going on with that pregnant teenage girl having seizures?"

"I don't have a clue, but I intend to ask Gavin to keep me in the loop."

"My theory is…" he wiped a bit of syrup from the corner of his mouth and swallowed before continuing "…the boyfriend gave her an ultimatum when he found out she was pregnant. Get rid of it or lose me. Maybe she couldn't go through with what he suggested."

She stopped in mid-bite and stared at him. Was there a hidden message in his words, or was he merely talking about the recent ER case? She wanted to ask him what his real point was, but wasn't sure she wanted to know the answer, so she swallowed the pancakes and reached for her coffee. "Don't know if we'll ever find out all of that information, but it's a possibility." Keep things superficial. Nonchalant. Why were her hands trembling? "Maybe she just found out she was pregnant and hoped he'd ask her to marry him?" Oops. There she went, referring to herself again. "But who can say? It's a different world out there these days."

"Tell me about it. One of our probationers recently filed sexual harassment charges toward his training officer."

"*His* training officer?"

"Yep. It was a woman doing the harassing, and evidently she'd made her plans for him very clear." He winked. "Most of the 'plans' were for after shift hours and involved little or no clothing. The guy thought he'd have to put out or risk getting a bad recommendation." Beck grinned.

"My, how the tables have turned." She smiled back.

For a millisecond she glimpsed their old friendship, how they'd tell each other secrets and discuss things that didn't make sense to them, and how each could trust the other when it came to figuring life out. And when they couldn't jointly come to a logical conclusion, which was most of the time, they would laugh.

Throughout her life she'd heard that a true test of friendship was when you could pick up right where you'd left off, no matter how long it'd been since you'd seen the other person. If Jan could take away all the other complications of the relationship between Beck and herself, she could admit that the rest, the friendship part, felt as though they'd never been apart.

Gooey warmth started in her chest and would have turned into a sappy longing for what they used to have, but she put an end to it with a quick reality check. *If he knew her secret he'd hate her.*

Lately, a new thought had been pushing its way into her conscience. Wishing she could put a sock in the mouth of the tiny voice in the back of her mind, she mentally stuck her fingers in her ears and sang *La, la, la, la*. It didn't help. The chant refused to be drowned out. Sooner or later she'd have to face the inevitable.

Beck deserves to know.

Shut up!

Fighting near panic, she diverted her attention. She chanced a glance his way and made an abrupt detour to the hollow of his neck, the spot she'd once loved to kiss. She'd kiss him gently there and watch the pulse speed up and feel amazed that she had that power over him. By the time her gaze met his eyes, he was watching her, carefully, as if he knew exactly what she'd just been thinking.

If he only knew the half of it. *Please, don't let him be a mind-reader.*

"You know what I always liked about you, January?"

Discomfort settled around her ribs. Did Beck need to go there? To tell her things she couldn't bear to hear ever again?

He didn't give her a chance to stop him. "You weren't one of those good-looking girls who were always checking themselves out in mirrors or windows. It was almost as if you didn't know how beautiful you were."

The ache in her chest twisted into an agonizing knot, and pressed against her lungs. *Please, don't do this to me. I can't handle it.*

She opted for fake cheeriness. "Well, you can't accuse me of being beautiful these days," she said, adjusting her glasses and nervously flipping her bobbed hair.

"Not so. You see, blonde highlights and long hair and sexy make-up, that's icing on the cake, sure. But real beauty is in here." He tapped his fist on his chest. "Sure, you were a knockout, but I got to know a much more beautiful girl than anyone else did."

"Please, don't do this, Beck…"

"Why not? We were too young when we first fell in love. Now we've matured. We're unattached. I still find you very attractive. Why not see if there's any spark left?"

He still found her attractive? A desert's worth of dryness filled her throat. She needed a drink of water. Shaking her head adamantly, she reached for the glass and sipped. She'd have to drown herself to quench the thirst. "Number one— we're working together, and number two—trying to relive the past is always a recipe for disaster."

His full lips disappeared into a thin line. His hazel stare cut through her defenses. He wadded his napkin up and tossed it on the table, then took the check and studied it. As he did, he said, "Are you seeing someone else?"

She gave a faint shake of her head. He slipped her a sideways glance and smiled. "What have you got to go home to at the end of the day?"

"That's none of your business, Beck. I think you're being too forward, and you're making me uncomfortable."

They reverted to one of their old stand-off stares. The same kind of deadlocked glaze they'd once given when they hadn't been able to agree on an issue. She'd end the discussion by calling him "Manimal" and he'd retort with "Fembot" then he'd chase her around and she'd pretend to fight him off, until finally she let him kiss her and they'd forget whatever they'd disagreed on.

Man, had things changed.

Something shifted in his eyes, as if he'd just relived the same scenario. "Then I apologize," he said curtly. He fished in the back pocket for his wallet and pulled out a small business card and a few bills. He left a couple of dollars on the table for a tip then used his fingers to clip the other to the check. "If you change your mind, this is my card." He separated the business card from the cash and handed it to her. She hesitated, but didn't want to be rude and took it. "There's my home phone number and my cell is underneath."

After he'd paid the bill, he walked her to the parking lot and, squinting from the sun, gave her a half-smile. Sparks seemed to leap off his skin and onto hers. She felt every single point of contact. This reaction to Beck wasn't about high school and old times, this was now and his sex appeal had fanned and caught like wildfire on her flesh. Her cheeks flushed hot.

"You have a good day off," he said, and swaggered away.

She stuttered but said goodbye and started toward her car. What *did* she have to go home to? Grocery shopping? A little house cleaning and then what? Dinner alone, with the company of a book, and, having spent time with Beck, a boatload of forgotten memories? And newly awakened desires she'd long forgotten she possessed.

She tucked his business card into her pocket and dug into her purse for the car keys. After turning down his blunt proposition, she was either the wisest woman on the earth or the biggest fool she'd ever met. Now all she had to do was figure out which.

Beck threw his leg over his bike and secured his helmet. He revved the engine and took off from the parking lot, gliding his foot lightly over the asphalt for balance. Frustration formed knots at the back of his neck. He had a thousand questions he'd meant to ask January, but hadn't uttered one of them. He wanted to get even with her for screwing up his life, yet any time he spent around her only made him want her more than ever.

He'd recently read an article written by a psychologist on the topic of the high-school reunion effect on rekindling old flames. The gist was that first loves were always the most powerful and often imprinted themselves on the two lovers' lives, similar to many species of birds that mated for life. The phenomenon, as the author described it, played out year after year as divorced adults rediscovered their first loves at a reunion and wound up finally marrying them.

He'd guffawed at the story when he'd first read it, but something had clicked in the back of his mind. He related to that "imprinted" feeling…with January.

He'd be a total fool to think something like that could happen with her. She'd just made it very clear their time together was ancient history. It was finally time to get over it.

But not before he got even.

Since he'd first hatched the plan, the thought of making her pay had definitely lost its appeal. All he had to do was look at her. Even a few pounds heavier and a lot less glitzy, January had his love-starved brain doing calisthenics. What fool came up with the saying men never made passes at girls who wore glasses? He'd already gotten used to her black, boxy frames. They suited the shape of her face, and even though she probably assumed she looked studious in them, he thought they made her spicier. What he especially liked was how her bob slipped from behind an ear and slanted across one eye. The darker ash blond shade was just as sexy as the old color. And when she used her slender fingers to sweep it away, well, what could he say? It sent an electrical current humming through his body.

To use an old saying, he could kill two birds with one stone. Revenge sex should answer the imprinting question.

After a quiet day on the job on Tuesday, and slipping into scrubs at the hospital, Beck glanced at Jan as she arrived at work. He approached with a broad smile, planning to take another risk and ask her for a date the coming week-end. He wasn't about to take no for an answer. How else was he going to get into her bed?

Jan hadn't changed into scrubs yet and she wore straight-legged jeans with copper-colored flats and a matching top. She'd also applied lipstick today, and that small addition made her beach-sky blue eyes nothing less than stunning from behind her heavy framed lenses.

He stalled in mid-stride and swallowed to get himself together.

"You're just the man I was looking for," she said, further derailing his train of thought.

"Yeah?" Nothing like snappy repartee to entice a lady.

"Yeah." She crossed her arms and tapped a foot. "I'll talk to you after I've changed," she said as she slipped into the ladies' dressing room.

Maybe she'd changed her mind about seeing him?

Beck hung around, feeling both optimistic and like a fool—a fool with a grudge and a plan to get even.

With a booming voice, Carmen announced an incoming major trauma patient via helicopter, and Gavin appeared at his office door and strode to Beck's side.

"We'll do this intake together," Gavin said.

Jan emerged from the locker room in uniform and Gavin added her to the team. "Jan, show Beck to the roof and transport the patient together."

She nodded.

As they made their way to the roof, Beck expected Jan to finish what she'd started to say earlier. Instead, he found she'd moved on to the weather and quizzing him about helicopter transports and the military. He didn't want to be pushy, so he let his curiosity take a back seat and answered her questions.

He'd make time to ask her for a date later.

"You know what this guy is here for, right?" she said.

He nodded.

"Motorcycle accident," she said, staring him down.

"Yep."

"Doesn't it make you wonder how long your luck will hold out?"

"I don't take risks," he said.

She sputtered a laugh.

"What?" He innocently raised his hands just as the helicopter came into view. He'd play the charming card until he got what he wanted.

The yellow helicopter circled the hospital. The flapping noise of the rotor blades intensified during the descent until Beck thought his ears would burst. A gale-force blast practically knocked them off their feet while the chopper landed.

Almost the instant the aircraft touched down, the door slid open and the flight EMT and attendant jumped out, lowering the patient, who was strapped onto a stretcher.

Jan led the way with the ER gurney and Beck pushed

along behind her. Her hair flipped and flapped against her head, looking like the spinning helicopter blades. Powerful wind pelted his face with sharp pinpricks of sensation. He raised his forearm and elbow to guard against the on-slaught, to no avail.

The EMT shouted something at them. Beck couldn't hear a thing beyond the rhythmic air-chopping beat. The sound threw him back in time to a battlefield and the cries for help, to decisions, right or wrong, that changed soldier's lives, some for better, others for worse. In a flash, memo-ries of life-threatening times resurfaced, where the tick of the clock hammered down on him. He tensed. Fine perspi-ration moistened his upper lip.

"Beck!" Jan grabbed his arm and pulled him forward. "Give us a hand."

He snapped out of his nightmarish thoughts.

The three worked in tandem to transfer the back-boarded, neck-braced, and extremity-splinted twenty-something patient from stretcher to hospital gurney in one smooth move. Though a practiced and swift transfer, the man still cried out in pain.

Both arms and the left leg were broken, according to the previously called-in report. There were also possible head and neck injuries, though the patient appeared to be fairly alert. After the transfer, they pushed the patient toward the locked hospital ER elevator at a quick clip.

Once inside the elevator the emergency medical flight technician gave them more detail. "He went down on the freeway, weaving between cars. Compound fractures of the right femur and left humerus and radius. Crushed tibia and fibula, right side, from passing car. Fractured right humerus.

Possible cervical and hip fractures. Peter, can you hear me?" the EMT called out to the semi-conscious patient.

A faint, hoarse voice replied. "Yeah."

Every bump and joggle of the gurney caused the patient to cry out in pain as they exited the elevator and rolled him closer to the ER. Sadistic as it seemed, Beck was glad to hear them as the man's cries were a good sign, proving he still had some fight left in him.

"Vital signs stable with elevated blood pressure 155 over 90, pulse 110, and respirations 24, with good oxygen levels."

Gavin met them at the entrance to the ER and the EMT repeated his information as they speed-walked the patient to an available procedure room. Gavin dismissed a medical student and a first-year ER resident who'd fallen in step with them. "We'll handle this one."

After a complete physical assessment of the patient, including a neuro check and a slew of verbal orders, including multiple X-rays, he glanced at Beck. "We need IV access to prep him for surgery and to give pain meds." He turned back to the patient. "You're not on blood thinners, are you?"

The guy mouthed, "no."

Gavin turned back to Beck. "With his compound fractures, he'll need antibiotic therapy, too."

Gavin walked Beck to the side of the room and lowered his voice. "You've done central venous line insertions, right, Beck?"

Beck turned his head and lowered his voice so the patient couldn't hear. "Only jugular sticks, and nothing like the procedure you do."

"You've seen me start a few of these babies the last couple of days. What's that saying? Watch one, do one, teach one?"

Beck raised his brows and nodded.

"That's what you're here for, right? To update and enhance your experience?"

"On the frontline our goal is to keep the patient alive long enough to get them transported to the field hospital. I can stick a jugular or femoral with the best of them, even do intra-osseous hydration, but this is out of my experience."

"You've got great hands. I've watched you. You can do this. You've watched one. Now it's time to do one. Next week you can teach the interns." Gavin smiled and winked. "Come on, I'll talk you through it," he went on in a raspy whisper.

Beck hesitated. If the central venous line wasn't inserted properly it could puncture the lung or the subclavian artery, which could cause hemorrhaging. Did he want to risk it for experience?

"Look, I've got five or six other guys chomping at the bit to do this. I'm offering it to you. It's your call."

Beck's first inclination was to let the intern or resident do the procedure, but the adventurous part of him, the part Gavin had just challenged, thought, Why not?

All Gavin had to do was look at Jan and on cue she went right to work gathering the supplies.

"And I'll give you my best nurse to assist. Hell, she could perform a subclavian in her sleep. She'll anticipate your every need, and I'm here as back up if you run into a problem."

Gavin was offering a once-in-a-lifetime chance. He decided to take it. Beck nodded and walked toward the gurney. He looked at the semi-conscious patient. The last thing he wanted to do was make matters worse for the guy, but Gavin believed in him and any experience here at Mercy Hospital was a bonus and could save a life in the field.

With the patient's neck in a cervical collar, the jugular approach was definitely out, which left the subclavian route, a procedure he was much less familiar with. His brain jumped to hyper-speed, running through the procedure he'd never actually performed himself but had observed frontline doctors and Gavin do.

Recalling how his advanced medic courses had made training even more challenging by first having the medics run a mile, dive under low shelters and start IVs in near darkness while holding the fluid bags with their teeth, he figured this couldn't be much more difficult. The jugular lines he'd trained on, though on sedated goats, had to be performed in equally chaotic circumstances while being timed with a stopwatch. And in the field the only way to check if you'd made it into the right vein was to lower the IV bag and check for backflow.

It would be a huge risk, but Gavin believed in his skills, and life was all about taking chances if you wanted to grow.

All things considered, the controlled atmosphere and bright lighting, with Gavin's back-up and Jan's assistance, this procedure should be far less complicated. Still, his confidence wavered and he took a deep breath to steady his hands. He used the only technique that ever got him through battles: tune out the rest of the world—focus on the patient, one procedure, and one chance at success.

OK. He was ready.

Beck cut open the patient's shirt and exposed the area he'd be working on. He washed his hands while January tilted the head of the bed slightly toward the floor to make sure the central veins were filled.

While he gowned up and put on gloves, Jan used the antimicrobial wash to cleanse the skin.

Jan also wore sterile gloves and she handed him the local anesthetic in a syringe with a small needle. He'd concentrate deep at the middle third of the clavicle to find the vein for cannulation, so he started superficially injecting the anesthetic there and worked outward along the entire length of the bone. Gavin nodded his approval.

Without having to ask, Jan handed him a longer needle and he injected a second round of medicine deeper into the flesh to ensure a pain-free procedure. Drawing on strict training, with each injection he aspirated to make sure he hadn't punctured the vein.

She handed him the guidewire and Gavin helped him check both the stiff and floppy ends while waiting for the anesthetic to numb the skin. He spoke quietly into Beck's ear, telling him the next step of the procedure.

Beck reached for the scalpel Jan provided and used it to nick the skin just enough to make sure the cannula would fit. He firmly palpated for the pulse, then used the introducer attached to a syringe and guided it carefully into the deep part of the clavicle, aiming toward the sternal notch.

He encountered resistance. The last thing he wanted was to run into trouble with an audience. He lifted his gaze toward his attending doctor.

Gavin spoke up. "Walk the introducer down just a bit." Beck complied. "That's it," Gavin said.

He followed Gavin's instruction until he had passed the blockage and could easily advance the introducer again. Steady suction on the attached syringe revealed a flush of blood when he entered the vein. He deftly removed the syringe from the introducer, feeling a bit like a circus juggler. Gavin had gloved up and reached in to help him handle the exchange. Beck used his thumb to prevent back-flush of blood from the introducer entrance.

Again, as though reading his mind, Jan was right there, handing him the guide wire to insert into the introducer. He took great care to make sure the wire didn't uncurl past the sterile field. Gavin hovered, ready to jump in if anything went wrong, and held a portion of the wire that threatened to touch outside the field.

Once satisfied he was in the right place, after checking the markers on the guide wire and leaving just a bit pro-truding from the insertion site, Beck glanced at Gavin, who nodded his approval.

"Looks right," Gavin said.

Beck removed the introducer over the guide wire. Jan handed him the cannula, already having removed the plastic end-stop, and he inserted it over the guide wire until it was level with the skin. Once confident all was well, and getting a nod of approval from Gavin, he removed the guide wire and left the cannula in place. He passed the withdrawn wire to Jan, who was waiting to receive it. In the field, he'd had to do everything in the procedures himself, and having her assistance was a luxury he greatly appreciated.

Jan had flushed the connecting line with saline and her steady hand reached toward his to attach it snugly to the cannula. A quick flash came to mind of the famous Michelangelo painting of The Hand of God where fingers almost touched. January was the only other person who knew about his passion for art. Hell, they'd discovered art together.

He quickly refocussed when she handed off the line and he connected it. When she passed him the needle and sutures, he took another breath, glad to see something that was easy for him to perform. He dutifully stitched the cannula in place flush to the skin through two separate holes in small plastic wings.

He let out his breath, not having been aware he'd been holding it, and allowed himself a mental pat on the back at a job well done. He passed a subtle smile January's way. She nodded her approval.

While he disposed of the extra suture and the needle, Jan cleaned and swabbed the skin and applied a small dressing.

Shortly after that the portable X-ray technician came to take a quick radiograph of the chest. They stepped outside and Gavin slapped him on the back.

"That was smooth," Gavin said. "Just like a pro. Have you ever thought about becoming a doctor?"

Beck laughed. "Never." He grinned but quickly stopped when he noticed the dagger looks from a couple of interns. He shifted and glanced at Jan down the hall, disposing of the equipment and trash. "She was a huge help."

Gavin grabbed his arm and pulled him closer. "The nurses here at Mercy are exceptional, and Jan is one of our best." He glanced with a mischievous twinkle in his eyes at Carmen. "Whatever you do, don't let her know I said that."

Beck chuckled and nodded. "Not a chance."

Gavin barreled toward the obviously unhappy interns. "Follow me to my office." They did what they were told.

Five minutes later the X-ray revealed that the subclavian line was in the right atrium instead of the superior vena cava. Beck had advanced it too far. Once again, under Gavin's tutelage, they went back to the patient, snipped the sutures and withdrew the line approximately 5 centimeters.

They took another X-ray, which revealed proper placement, before suturing the line in place again.

Shortly thereafter the patient was transferred to surgery and Gavin once again arranged for Beck to scrub in and observe.

Excited about the OR opportunity, Beck couldn't help being a bit disappointed when he realized he wouldn't be seeing Jan again the rest of the shift. She'd teased him earlier and he was hoping for that shot at another date, but now it would have to wait.

Taking the hallway steps two at a time, rather than wait for the notoriously slow elevator, Beck was halfway to the second-floor surgery suites when his cellphone rang.

It was Jan.

CHAPTER FIVE

FULLY submerged in the extra-long bathtub, Jan stared through the water toward the ceiling. Everything looked distorted and dreamlike. The thick silence brought her peace and helped tamp down the growing apprehension in her gut. She wanted to inhabit this other-worldly place for as long as her breath could hold.

Beck would arrive at 7 p.m. tonight, her Friday night off, and he deserved to know about their child. How exactly was a person supposed to casually tell someone long after the fact, "Thanks for stopping by and, oh, yeah, we had a baby together twelve and a half years ago."

She emerged through the water's surface into a sitting position, gasping for air, with her hair dripping down her neck and her heart pounding against her sternum. What had she been thinking when she'd invited him over?

She pulled the plug and stood, wrapping herself in a huge bath towel. In her bedroom, her citrus flower-patterned top and cropped pants lay waiting across the bed. What was appropriate to wear on an event of this magnitude? A flash of black funeral attire appeared in her mind.

Beck deserved to know the truth, but would she have nerve enough to tell him tonight?

An hour and a half later she put the finishing touches on the simple dinner she'd prepared. The chicken, artichoke hearts and rice casserole in the oven smelled inviting, but the tennis-ball-sized knot in her stomach promised to keep her from enjoying a single bite. She paced the kitchen, chewing a fingernail, mumbling her over-rehearsed version of how and why she'd never told Beck about their baby.

I knew how important your dream of seeing the world was, and I'd only found out I was pregnant the day before you were to leave. I couldn't bear ruining your chance of leaving Atwater for good, and I didn't want you to be distracted during bootcamp.

The excuse sounded flimsy and lame to her, so how would it sound to him? If he gave her the chance to say more, she'd tell him the role her mother had played in the final decision. First she'd reminded Jan how hard her own life had been as a single mother. She'd thrown statistics in her face about poverty and teenage pregnancy. Then she'd sworn she wasn't going to tie her life up raising a grandkid, and had told her that thirty-four was far too young to be a grandmother. She'd pleaded with January to consider her future, the career in entertainment she'd always dreamed about. "How can you show up at auditions with a child groping at your legs?" When Jan had suggested that maybe Beck's parents would help out, her mother scoffed. "You want your baby raised in the house of an alcoholic child abuser? That bastard father of his beats the hell out of Beck."

Jan was such a dreamer she'd never had any idea Beck was being abused. She'd always believed him when he'd shown up bruised and abraded and said he'd been in a fight. She'd naively assumed it went along with his bad-boy persona. Never did she fathom his own father was the beast he'd battled. No wonder he couldn't wait to get away.

It didn't take long for Karen to realize that she hadn't weakened Jan's resolve, so she lied and blackmailed her daughter into thinking Beck could go to jail for having sex with a minor. She called it statutory rape and said it didn't matter that the sex had been consensual. Too young, frightened, and, let's face it, dumb to know the reality of "unlawful sexual intercourse," she did what her mother said. Years later, on a hunch, she researched it and found it was only a misdemeanor and a fine, and rarely did police arrest teens for consensual sex. Only in extreme age differences and with females fourteen or younger did they pursue the males. Knowing Jan would defend Beck at all costs, her mother had lied about the law and manipulated her once again. When she'd finally confronted her mother about it, Karen laughed it off and reiterated, "It was for your own good." Jan didn't talk to her for an entire year after that. Then her mother married and moved away.

Was there a chance that Beck would buy her pitiful excuse for robbing him of a major decision in his life? Maybe if she killed him with kindness and used the old velvet-hammer approach she'd survive the night. At this stage in life she didn't dare hope for forgiveness, just closure.

Riding a surprisingly strong wave of disappointment, she accepted that after tonight she'd cure Beck of wanting to rekindle their old friendship. Hell, he'd never want to see her again.

The doorbell rang. She bit through her fingernail with a loud click, making her tooth hurt.

Beck stood on the doorstep and sniffed, hoping he hadn't overdone his aftershave. The last thing he wanted was to be obvious about his intentions. He'd had to change his day off to be here, even worked all last night and half of this morning to make things work out. Thanks to his fatigue, he'd depend on adrenaline to carry him through tonight. He'd purposely steered clear of Jan all week, choosing to pick up his ER hours during the day shift on his days off instead of coming in evenings. Spending too much time around her confused him, and he needed to stay focussed.

Long ago, on his first leave from the military, he'd come back for her and she'd disappeared. Karen Stewart's stone-faced lie hadn't fooled him. He'd known she'd had plans for her daughter and hadn't wanted her hooking up with him, a loser, but he'd loved her and deserved to know where she was. Then he'd gotten the call.

Beck worked the muscle in his jaw so hard it threatened to cramp. If he could keep his conscience from messing up his plans, the evening promised to be an adventure. Revenge sex. Hmm. It had a nice ring to it.

The door opened and a burst of color in the form of Jan's scoop-neck blouse took him by surprise. She'd put on make-up, too, and on that pretty face the effect was staggering. But the thing that knocked him off balance was the obviously missing glasses, and the shining, sea-blue eyes looking directly at him. Those same eyes used to plunge deep into his soul. A pang of longing threatened a desire to abort his plan. He shrank back a bit, wondering if she could still read his mind like she used to.

Beck looked away, pretending to be distracted by the passing car with muffler problems.

"Hi," she said, sounding breathy.

"Hey," he said, returning his gaze to the lure of her eyes. *Think of something to say, idiot.* "These flowers match your top." He reached into his leather jacket and handed her a small bouquet, which was slightly battered from being stuffed inside. Riding a motorcycle wasn't always convenient, yet he'd purposely decided to ride instead of drive his car tonight. It felt more in tune with his intentions.

Jan gave a pleased smile, sniffed the bouquet, and stepped aside so he could enter.

Stay on point, he scolded himself when he softened at the sight of her living room. If he'd had to imagine what the new January's condo would look like, this would be it. Neatly upholstered furniture, splashes of colorful pillows and throw rugs and carefully chosen paintings reflected this cautious woman, as opposed to the free-spirited girl he'd once been in love with. Cautious because she'd been kicked in the teeth by life? A small ache in his chest made him wish he could go back in time. But this woman, the new January, had awakened the sleeping giant, and he'd found himself yearning for something more. No longer fluff and flash, she'd matured into substance and reality, and it only made her more attractive.

But he had a mission tonight.

While she tended to the flowers, his eyes came to rest on a glass box perched on a bookshelf.

Immediately recognizing the object almost threw his breathing out of kilter. Inside the small glass case was an acrylic painted paisley egg on a tiny stand. The eggshell he'd designed in the elective art class he'd taken on a dare in eleventh grade. The class where he'd first met January. They'd eyed each other for half the semester. Being the school social queen, she'd gone on and on about how talented he was when she'd seen his mid-term project. She'd giggled about her own clumsy pattern, and compared it to his "work of art," as she'd called it. He'd never done anything artistic before, but he'd enjoyed every day of that class, especially after finding January. Her encouragement, along with the teacher's, had given him the courage to explore a whole new side of his personality—the artistic side. Or the pansy side, as his father used to deride him. Art was a secret pleasure he enjoyed and kept hidden from his coworkers to this very day.

For someone who'd dropped him the minute he'd left town, it seemed odd that she'd keep the egg he'd used to bribe her into going out with him that first time. The eggshell, as delicate as their love, had not only been kept but had been enshrined on a pedestal in a glass box.

She whisked back into the room. He glanced up to find a sheepish expression in her eyes. He didn't want to put her on the spot, or to stir up old emotions, not on his night of revenge, so he removed his fingertips from the top of the glass box and didn't mention the egg.

"Something smells great," he said, reverting back to flirt-on-a-mission mode.

She smiled, obviously grateful for the distraction. "I hope you're hungry. It's a special recipe."

That would be just like January, and, nope, he wasn't going to let the fact that she'd made something special for him get in the way of his goal. As he followed her into the other room, he tried to figure out if being seriously turned on was off limits with revenge sex.

Standing in her kitchen, inhaling the delicious smell of baking chicken and savory spices, certainly increased his senses, which seemed to be putting him in the mood... faster than he cared to admit. But revenge sex was supposed to be cold and, calculated and above all, manipulating. And he was supposed to be totally in control. He'd never actually had revenge sex before, but that was how he imagined it should be.

Damn. Why had he noticed that egg? And, oh, no, she was putting on a cute and frilly apron that said, "Kiss the cook." How was he supposed to get ruthlessly even with the happy homemaker materializing before him?

She handed him a glass of wine, and he didn't have the heart to tell her he didn't like wine. So he thanked her, took a sip, and tried not to pucker his lips at the dry tartness.

Maybe he'd put his revenge scenario on hold until after dinner, then he'd steel himself against her sweet gestures and soft, round curves and concentrate on cold, hard sex as he lured her into her bedroom.

She passed him a plate of spring rolls, his favorite since forever, and actually batted her eyelashes at him. Was she flirting, too?

"Could you carry this into the other room?" she asked, gathering two small saucers of dipping sauce and following behind with appetizer plates and a wad of napkins.

They wound up facing each other on the neatly upholstered couch, sharing the best-tasting spring rolls he'd had in years.

"You didn't get these from that place we used to hang out at, did you?"

She shook her head. "No. But I found this ma-and-pa restaurant nearby that makes spring rolls almost as good."

"Almost? Nah. These are the exact same recipe. You've got to tell me where they're located."

"Sure." She smiled and he thought the wine must have gone to his head, except he hadn't taken another sip since the first horrible taste.

He dipped and popped another spring roll into his mouth. How in the hell was he going to pull off his plans? After a few more crunchy chews, as contentment settled in, he didn't much care.

Jan had carefully removed every picture of Meghan from the living room and placed them in her bedroom for safekeeping. She'd even closed the door, something she never did, but her room was next to the only bathroom in the condo and she couldn't take the chance of him seeing them.

Something strange had happened since Beck had arrived. New energy thrummed through her veins just from being in the same room with him. Her jitters had calmed down, too, and she was actually enjoying his company, just like the good old days, but that was no surprise.

He'd worn a classic crew-necked pullover sweater in deep forest green, which made his eyes even more striking. The last thing she wanted to do was stare, but she couldn't stop looking into those dark and mysterious pools. And when he smiled, like he was doing right now, he still looked like a gentle little boy posing for a school picture. Damn, she was easy. Forcing her gaze away, she studied how he'd pushed the thin sleeves of the silk knit up his brawny forearms and how angular his hands were. Maybe that wasn't such a good idea either. She nibbled on her spring roll and pretended to be fascinated with the small bean sprouts stuffed inside.

How odd to be sitting across from the guy she'd thought she'd die over when she'd had to give him up. Yet here they were, sharing spring rolls and chattering on about all the silly things they used to do, as if the world they'd once known hadn't come to an abrupt end. And an innocent baby hadn't been sent to strangers to be raised.

"Remember that time someone set off firecrackers under the bleachers during a football game and everyone assumed it was me?" An ironic grin spread across his face.

"You used to get blamed for everything." She shook her head, remembering how unjust the principal had been.

"But not that time." A mischievous twinkle started in his gaze and trickled down to the smirk dancing on his lips.

As the significance sank in, Jan felt a rush of warmth release and spread up her neck to her cheeks. "I was your alibi!"

He nodded. "Exactly. You finally had to come out of the closet and admit that we were going out."

"I wasn't ashamed of us."

"Right. Let's just say your reputation changed overnight from being Miss Popularity Queen to Chopper Chick."

Unable to resist, she laughed. "It did not." Many of her so-called friends had dropped her after the news had spread about who she was dating. Turned out they hadn't *really* been friends.

He gave her that challenging, sexy stare that used to drive her nuts, the look that reached inside and jumbled every single sane thought. Damn, he was handsome. An overwhelming urge to run her hand over the fine stubble of his closely shaven head made her sit straighter and fist her hands.

"You got knocked off your pedestal so fast you probably thought we'd had an earthquake." His teasing gaze probed deep into hers. "Before you knew it, you were hanging with the outsiders."

The truth was, she didn't care who she'd hung out with as long as Beck had been there. He'd made her feel safe and accepted in any situation, and he'd opened her heart to the biggest adventure of her life—love. As crazy as a loon, go-for-it-and-never-look-back love. She sighed…and covered by pretending the spring roll was the most delicious thing she'd ever tasted.

This new version of Beck was even more enticing. All man, he could enter a room and immediately lure her in as though connected by an invisible string. The string of their past. Yet what she saw in the here and now was more than she'd ever allowed herself to dream of when they'd been kids. He seemed steady and dependable and a man she could trust.

His eyes drifted from her face toward her blouse, then, as though thinking better of it, his gaze climbed back up to hers.

If he kept looking at her in that way, like she was the sexiest woman alive and he hadn't been with a woman in years, she'd break into a sweat right in front of him. A foreign liquid-warm awareness stirred deep inside and put her on edge. "I'd better check on our dinner," she said, standing up quickly, running from the persuasive gravity of Beck.

He followed her into the kitchen. "Anything I can do?"

Put him to work. Get him away from you. While opening the oven and using oven pads to check the casserole, she nodded toward the dishes she'd placed on the counter. "You can set the table."

He washed his hands, picked up the dishes and left for the tiny dining room.

The pulse that had been picking up speed in her neck settled enough for her to lift the dish without dropping it. But the new energy thrumming through her limbs wouldn't let her forget that Beck Braxton was in her house and he still had "it".

How in the world would she make it through the evening?

They'd had a great dinner, catching up on all the silly things they'd been up to, and Beck felt a surge of progress when January kicked off her shoes over coffee and dessert in the living room. He glanced around, wishing she had a fireplace, but no such luck. After catching sight of the painted egg again, curiosity got the better of him.

"Why'd you save it?" He nodded toward the bookcase, though she obviously knew what he'd referred to.

Jan grew quiet, as though figuring out how to explain it. Her clear blue eyes clouded, as if myriad memories flew by. They brightened, sparkled, dimmed, and looked pained, all within a single second. A tiny twitch of her brow made him worry she might cry, but the crease soon softened and she smiled warmly at him.

"I guess that eggshell represented all the possibilities I

felt, being with you." A furtive gaze drifted quickly past his face. Her wistful smile widened. "And it was beautiful because you made it and you didn't even know how talented you were."

A ball of warmth hit his chest with a thud. So much for retribution. Suddenly he didn't care what phoney revenge he'd told himself he'd come to carry out tonight. He edged closer to her on the couch.

"Besides," she said, lifting her chin, "you gave it to me, and it's not polite to give gifts away."

He noticed a sudden hurt flicker in her gaze, and longed to ease whatever pain lived inside her. Something else became apparent. Every atom in his body still craved Jan and he couldn't stop himself from touching her. He reached for her jaw and gently fingered the soft flesh of her earlobe. She didn't resist his touch, but instead leaned into his palm and trained her wide-eyed stare on him. There it was, that same look she used to flash at him, as though she was trying to trust him.

He'd never trust her again. Remember? This was just sex. Get her out of your system. Go on with your life.

Her delicate nostrils flared almost imperceptibly. He bent forward and nuzzled her cheek with his nose, inhaling the scent of her skin and hair and releasing the last of his restraint.

Memories, as if a life force, flooded his mind, guiding him closer to Jan. Not sensing the least bit of resistance from her, he lightly rubbed his nose against the tip of hers, and felt her sigh an airy breath over his lips.

She tilted her head, her mouth searched for his, and his lips danced briefly over hers. A faint thrill was all he could afford to release right now. Needing to get a grip, he pulled back and gazed into her soft, dreamy stare. Instead of coming to his senses, he wanted nothing more than to go there…with her. Now.

This wasn't the right mind set, but it was useless to try to change. A faint groan escaped his throat when he allowed himself the pleasure and his mouth covered hers. The pads of her lips were warm and moist and he couldn't help himself. He pressed harder against her softness and opened her lips, soon finding his way inside to the velvet of her mouth. He inhaled with her, and rediscovered kisses and tastes he'd long missed but had never forgotten. But there was something more. Now he kissed a fully grown woman, the woman his first love had become. She was solid and sexy, and he tightened his grip on her arms to keep her near.

There was only one direction for them now. Forward.

Their tongues twined, and her arms snaked around his torso. She clutched him tight. He leaned back on the couch and stretched out his legs, bringing her along with him. His hands found her hips and placed them flush with his. No longer a slim teenager, she had a little more to grab these days, and he liked it. He liked this woman.

Responding to the feel of her body next to his, a firm, distinctive difference between them couldn't be ignored.

She lifted her head and gaped at him with a knowing look, a swath of hair covering one of her eyes. He saw as much fire in her gaze as he felt simmering in every cell of his body.

Never one to dawdle, especially when on a mission, he made a snap decision.

"Let's get naked on the couch." His gruff whisper drew chills along her neck, before he warmed it with his kisses.

Something must have clicked with Jan, too, because she smiled and said, "That sounds like a fantastical idea," then lowered herself onto his chest.

He took all of her weight as she stretched her arms along both sides of his head and nipped at his ear. Though he'd shaved before coming over, he wondered if his stubble scratched her face. If it did, she couldn't have cared because she rubbed her cheek against his several more times. Tingles marched down his chest, strengthening his need.

He clenched his arms around her back and waist, holding her as close as possible, savoring the feel of every inch of her, this new yet familiar woman. Damn, he'd missed her and he definitely liked what he'd rediscovered. No one else had ever felt as right in his arms as January. He captured her mouth and kissed her long and hard. She answered each kiss with several of her own, driving him mad with mounting desire. To hell with revenge sex. He *wanted* to be with her. One more kiss and he'd never be able to turn back.

"Are you sure about this?" he managed to utter.

Beck's raspy whisper drew her out of her spell. Where was she? She'd been close to heaven one second before, then his throaty voice and fiery eyes had brought her back to earth. Dear God, what was she doing? She'd wanted to butter him up with dinner and conversation, while hoping to get up enough nerve to tell him what he deserved to know, but this bordered on seduction. Who was she kidding? This *was* seduction. But who was seducing whom?

They'd resorted to old habits of kissing leading to groping, and if history were to repeat itself, getting naked would soon follow. But this wasn't some sort of reliving of the past, this would be sex with a new and improved man. A man she wished she could know better.

Naked with Beck?

He'd already asked and she'd agreed!

This wasn't right, but it felt so good. It had been so long, and he felt perfect. Maybe after they took the edge off with mind-boggling sex Beck would be more open to hearing what must be said. Oh, God, the thought almost chased her libido into hiding…until she looked back into the eyes that only saw and wanted her, right now. Hopefully he'd come prepared.

"January," he whispered. "Are you sure about this?"

She hesitated, a zillion doubts rushing through her mind. "Y-yes," she said, before one more thought or slight hesitation could drive her off course.

"Whew." He smiled, sexy and seductive. "For a second there I thought you were going to change your mind."

She answered with a deep kiss and a full body press, wishing her clothes would disappear.

"First," he said, "we get rid of this." He reached for her shirt and raised it above her head in record time. The lacy yellow push-up bra soon joined the blouse on the floor, but not before he'd enjoyed the sight of her with glazed, hooded eyes and a deep guttural sound of approval.

"You're so beautiful," he said.

Excitement rushed over her when he lifted and kissed each breast, suckling until the nipples pearled tight and made her itch for more skin-to-skin contact. Making a quick break, he removed his clothes faster than her next breath while she peeled off her slacks.

For one heartbeat they went completely still and stared

at each other. She'd never seen a more beautiful man in her life. She prayed he wasn't disappointed with her, but when she looked into his eyes, all her worries vanished.

The look on his face was a combination of lust and awe, and she remembered seeing that same expression every time they'd ever made love. "You still take my breath away," he said in a hoarse whisper.

The phrase knocked the breath out of her and nearly made her cry. Unable to answer, she reached for him. They came together again in a tight embrace. Being flesh to flesh almost made her dizzy with sensation. She was with Beck, the love of her life, and he'd kissed her alive again. Longing to quench the awakening between her legs, she slid her hips down his body and caressed his tall erection with her thighs, moaning with delight at the feel of him. Smooth. Hard. Pulsing close to her core. Passion nipped in her belly as if a flame, and moisture blossomed in readiness between her legs.

Just short of lightning-bolt speed, he repositioned her on her back on the narrow couch. His hands ran down to her hips, ready to remove the last barrier between them. He slid the lacy panties over her toes and once at the foot of the sofa he gave a seductive, drop-dead grin before tossing them over his shoulder.

He was beautiful, sexier than any man alive, and she wanted him more than her next breath. If memory served her right, he had something else in mind first. As a foolish schoolgirl, he'd actually convinced her that this little trick of his wasn't having sex. She smiled, remembering. Oh, but she begged to differ.

As he smoothed his hands up her thighs, she tensed in

crazy longing, super-sensitive to his touch. He tongued her navel, setting off a rocket of heat. He peppered her stomach with delicate kisses she could barely endure. Shivers and tingles gently tortured her. The kissing trail moved lower, and her pulse thrummed stronger and harder as tension coiled deep inside. She reacted to him, as she always had, more intensely than anyone on earth. As he kissed her lower and lower she dug fingers into his surprisingly soft hair and held him tightly.

Jan arched and gasped with a sudden burst of sensation when he opened her with his tongue and over the next several minutes methodically released the pent-up pressure he'd exacted by his touch. Flashing memories of making love with Beck accompanied her heightening pleasure. But this wasn't a memory. He was here in the flesh and driving her crazy. In record time a deep noise erupted from her throat as lava-hot fireworks shot up and down her spine and out to her fingertips, before curling her toes.

They were together and nothing else seemed to matter. Confusion caused moisture to prickle behind Jan's eyelids when she closed her eyes and gave in to the magnitude of raw emotion. She hoped Beck wouldn't notice.

As she recovered from her orgasm, he slid on protection and entered her. She greedily reached for him, holding him as close as humanly possible while engulfed in more bitter-sweet memories. She let them go and thought only of Beck. Right here. Right now. Soon lost in the tight and controlled muscles of his back, arms and buttocks, she chased away all remorse. His strong thrusts drove her toward another release in record time. No longer feeling like the schoolgirl who'd wanted nothing more than to please him, she answered every move of his with her own. She'd give as well as take, and savor the feel of him inside and out, solid and hot. Real.

Time was suspended, and the world with all of its worries disappeared while they made love. Not one other thought resided in her mind but Beck and the wondrous sensations he gave her.

Deep inside, he found her most responsive spot and brought her to the brink again. Sensing his time was near, she searched for and found his mouth and kissed him hungrily until, at last, sensory overload brought them both to the edge…and over.

CHAPTER SIX

THE next morning Beck scratched his jaw and staggered into the kitchen with a broad smile on his face. He'd shown up last night determined to get revenge by using Jan for sex. Instead, they'd had a fantastic time and he'd given up on his cruel plan. Turned out it was a great idea because now he'd been rewarded by finally getting to sleep an entire night with her! No falling half-asleep and setting the alarm on his watch then scrambling to get dressed before her curfew, like back in high school.

They actually hadn't had much sleep. Doing the near impossible, his smile stretched even wider.

He'd left her sleeping in a pile of sheets with a clear conscience. To hell with revenge sex, it could never measure up. What they'd done last night had far surpassed anything they'd experienced as teenagers, and they'd spent a hell of a lot of time experimenting back then.

Sweet January—his favorite pin-up girl.

Hold on. She wasn't worthy of his trust. No matter how great the sex was, he'd stand guard.

Searching in the refrigerator for some eggs and cheese, he noticed a small magnet frame with a happy child's face peering out at him when he closed the door. He'd failed to notice it last night when surrounded by fantastic aromas and with the full distraction of Jan wearing an apron that said "Kiss the cook" on it.

He closed the door and studied the picture more closely. *Cute as a button. Must be a friend's kid.* Ah, but he had breakfast to prepare.

To the best of his recollection, Jan liked cheese omelets as much as pancakes, and since his cooking skills were limited, he'd make the one thing he knew would impress her. Why he wanted to impress the woman who still hadn't told him why she'd run out on him thirteen years ago, he wasn't sure. But since it was his goal to find out, an impressive cheese omelet it would be.

While scrabbling in a drawer for a spatula he heard the faint ringing of his cellphone and was on his way to answer it when the best thing he'd seen all morning showed up.

January.

To hell with the phone. He'd check the voice message later.

"Fancy meeting you here," he said, skimming his fingers along her neck and thinking how smooth her skin was.

"I was hoping you hadn't left," she said, accepting his peck on the cheek.

"Why would I leave?" *This is the best I've felt in ages.*

"I don't know. Hey, is that an omelet I smell?"

He nodded and waggled his eyebrows as though that said it all. Yes, he was her dream lover and personal chef. Payment in kisses would be accepted after the meal.

She'd obviously stopped in the bathroom to freshen up. Her skin was bright and fresh and her hair had been combed. Her simple nightgown called out to be removed.

Immediately.

The spark of his sexy idea got doused by the loud snap and sizzle of butter in the frying pan.

"The coffee's ready," he said, shifting back to chef duty and wondering why she was being a little elusive.

"Hey, why don't we add the leftover asparagus from last night?" she said.

OK, so she wanted to keep things superficial. He could do casual, if that was how she wanted it. "Sounds great to me."

She opened the refrigerator door while he flipped the fluffy eggs and sprinkled shredded Cheddar cheese over the center. He'd wait until she chopped the asparagus and added it before folding the omelet in half.

He was about to ask her about the cute little munchkin on the refrigerator when he looked up and noticed the picture was missing. Odd.

Jan sautéed the chopped asparagus without uttering a word, and Beck removed the pan from the stove while he waited for her contribution. Where had the responsive and welcoming woman from last night gone, and what was going on in her head?

She scooped the vegetables over the eggs and cheese and he did the honors of folding and sliding the omelet out of the pan and onto a plate. Still no conversation.

Maybe she was as amazed as he was at the sudden turn in their lives, and she'd been dumbstruck. Though the look on Jan's face as she ate communicated deep thoughts, and her usual sky-blue eyes seemed shrouded with concern rather than amazement. Great. He'd set himself up for rejection again by sleeping with her. Yet he was the one who was supposed to get even.

Had he only imagined how incredible their love-making had been last night? Nah, he couldn't have conjured up anything as fantastic even if he tried. Maybe she suspected he'd want some answers now that they'd been intimate again. Maybe she knew he expected some answers. Well, she was right, and if she ever wanted him to trust her again, she'd better open up.

Soon, sharing from a single plate, they were down to the last bite. Too bad if she didn't want to talk about things. He needed to know. Beck couldn't hold back the burning question in his heart another moment. "When I came home for leave, were you really in modeling school?"

Nothing short of panic registered in her eyes, though she quickly hid it. Years ago, he'd spent months trying to figure out what had gone wrong between them. He'd finally come to the conclusion that she hadn't been able to handle being close to him and having him leave, so she'd run away from him.

All he'd ever talked about had been adventure and his desire to see the world. Where would a woman, or a seventeen-year-old girl, fit into that plan? *Don't try to see it her way or let your guard down. She owes you some answers.*

Beck was due to ship out on a six-month tour of duty after his month at Mercy Hospital. Jan knew that. They'd gotten a hell of a lot closer last night than he'd ever expected. Was she thinking history was going to repeat itself? Maybe it was too much for her. He gazed back into her startled face, retreat already apparent in her eyes.

Jan had been carefully guarding her thoughts about how important it was to tell Beck the truth. And the sooner the better. She'd pretended that she'd enjoyed the eggs, and that they'd been tasty and light instead of bitter. When he'd hit her with the direct question about their past, the sour taste of bile had risen up the back of her throat.

She'd felt so devious slipping the forgotten magnet picture from the refrigerator and hiding it in the gadget drawer when he hadn't been looking. What kind of deceitful person had she turned into? And now he'd flat out asked the one question she feared the most.

They'd had one extraordinary night together. Could she dare hope for more with the huge secret looming like a dark cloud over their heads? The optimistic side of her hoped she could build on this new energy springing to life between them before she told him the whole story. But how long would he settle for bits and pieces before he'd grow frustrated and angry at her evasiveness?

She swallowed back the bitter taste. "I moved up north."

She dreaded what his next question would be, knowing she didn't have any response that wouldn't be an out-and-out lie. Could she lie to Beck again?

"Why?" He uttered the last question in the world she wanted to face.

Her shoulders slumped and her eyes closed. She inhaled, praying for strength. She'd already told him her stock answer about modeling school. He hadn't bought it.

His cellphone rang a decidedly odd jingle, the Monday night televised football theme, and cut through the extended silence.

Beck's eyes grew wary, his expression sharpened. "I've got to answer that. It's the SWAT team tactical alert ring."

He tore out of the kitchen, leaving Jan alone to calm her shaking hands and galloping heart.

A moment later he reappeared. "I've got to go. There's a bank robbery with hostages going down in Silverlake. All SWAT units have been called in."

He dressed fast but slowed down long enough to take Jan into his arms and kiss her breathless at the door. His morning stubble prickled her lips and cheeks, and sent shivers across her shoulders. He delved into her eyes, making her fear he could read the terror in her mind, seeing not only her secret but her new-found concerns for his safety.

"We'll pick up this conversation later," he said, then kissed her forehead before he left.

With a heavy heart she watched him jog toward his motorcycle and worried about what awaited him on the streets. She wanted Beck to be safe and come back to her even though she knew the very next time they were together she'd have to tell him everything.

She owed it to him.

"Be careful!" was all she could manage to call after him.

By the time Jan arrived at work that afternoon, every TV in every single emergency patient room had the live news coverage blaring out about the ongoing botched bank robbery and the subsequent hostage situation. Carmen gave a blow-by-blow narrative of the situation to the other nurses. Even Gavin seemed fascinated by the modern-day Bonnie and Clyde situation.

"They're releasing two more hostages," Carmen announced. "That leaves six. Wouldn't you love to hear the negotiations?"

"No," Jan said, biting back her anxiety and trying instead to focus on her job. At least there hadn't been any gunfire or loss of life as yet. A wave of butterflies stretched their wings in her stomach. She grabbed a patient chart and went into the only patient room without the TV on, hoping to distract herself. A few minutes later, in the middle of starting an IV, she heard the pop, pop, pop of televised gunfire, and the newscaster's hushed voice suddenly call out, "Things have escalated into an old-fashioned gunfight. There's a man down. No. Two."

Jan rushed to the door to see the nearest TV. The reporter and cameraman had obviously run for cover while filming a shaky newscast.

The studio anchor took over. "It appears that two people have been shot. It's not clear if the wounded are the bank robbers or the hostages."

More pop-pop-popping broke out, but this time it sounded like fireworks. Jan forced herself back to the patient's bedside and finished attaching the IV with a shaky hand and started the IVAC machine to deliver the fluid at 125 cc an hour. Her mind whirled with thoughts, each more horrendous than the last.

Always so drawn out in movies, the tense real-life drama had already come to an end by the time she'd returned to the nurses' station. Several bodies were strewn around the ground in front of the bank. The same on-the-scene reporter yapped on about the chaos and possible loss of life. He described the pools of blood and the grim atmosphere in breathless tones.

Jan strained to hear if any of the police officers involved had also been injured and got woozy with fear for Beck.

"Two SWAT guys got shot!" Carmen reported, glancing toward Jan with concern in her eyes. "Is Beck there?"

Jan clutched the counter to keep from swaying, and nodded.

Gavin strode toward the nurses' station, brows furrowed above serious dark eyes. "Discharge anyone who isn't an emergency," he said to the residents and other doctors. "We're going to need all our manpower for the casualties." He turned to Carmen. "Notify surgery. Get the triage stations ready to go. As of now, we're on Code Orange."

An hour later the ER was overrun with multiple incoming casualties and swarming with EMTs and policemen. Jan assisted a third-year resident as she placed a chest tube in one of the wounded hostages guilty of nothing more than being in the wrong place at the wrong time. Once she'd taped the tube in place, they rolled the gurney toward the back of the ER where the orderly waited with a nurse to transport the patient to the ER holding area while waiting for surgery.

Jan glanced up in time to see a group of SWAT officers dressed in full military-style gear from navy-blue jumpsuits with metal helmets to protective Kevlar vests and heavy-duty combat boots. They'd just brought in one of their own. Frantic, Jan searched the gurney to see if it was Beck.

She heard her name and turned. There he was, standing before her, surprisingly clean-looking for someone who'd just been involved in that kind of incident. Her heart doubled its rhythm. He wrapped his hand around her wrist and tugged her down the hall toward the utility kitchen as she tried to catch her breath. Once inside, she fell into his arms in a rush of relief and confusion. She buried her face against the steel of his bulletproof vest, surprised that the covering material was soft, and languished there while she tried to make sense of things. His arms wrapped her tight, offering momentary security.

"I was scared to death you'd been shot," she whispered.

"Not even close." He kissed the top of her head. "But my partner took a bullet in the abdomen, just below his vest, and he's in bad shape."

"Where is he?"

"We just brought him in. Gavin's taking care of him. The sooner they get him to surgery the better his chances."

"Let me go help," she said, breaking away.

He stopped her and pulled her back long enough to kiss her. The amazing feel of his lips on hers steadied her nerves better than any sedative could have. She lingered to enjoy his taste and smiled against his mouth as a quick buzz thrummed through her body. She could tell he felt it, too. But, then, they'd always shared something extraordinary.

Thank God Beck hadn't been injured.

Two in the morning Jan tossed and turned, trying to settle down her nerves and allow her over-stimulated brain and extra-fatigued body to rest. They'd worked non-stop in the ER stabilizing patient after patient from the bank robbery. Ten in all. Both bank robbers were dead, and six hostages had been wounded, along with the two SWAT officers. The last she'd heard, Beck's partner had pulled through surgery, though he'd wound up with a partial colectomy and was in the ICU. His condition was still touch and go and would remain so for several days, but she prayed he'd make it and be able to go home to his family.

Life would be a never-ending prayer of concern if she were to be with Beck again. If not his military service, his police duties would always be a barrier between them. She couldn't live with the constant worry any more than he could put up with her secrets. The sooner she told him about Meghan, the sooner he'd be out of her life…again.

She punched her pillow into submission and heard a faint tapping on her front door. Before she could respond, her phone rang. She answered on the first ring.

"It's me," Beck said. "Let me in."

Scrambling out of bed, she rushed toward the door. There Beck stood in civilian clothes looking worn out but outrageously handsome.

He flashed his famous smile. Long dimples cut deep into his cheeks. "May I come in?"

She stepped aside. "Of course." Her heart raced at the sight of him, but more so because of what she knew she needed to do. He didn't give her a chance to take a breath.

"It felt a little too much like war out there today. I keep expecting more gunfire or a car bomb. I was hanging out in ICU with some of the other guys, but went home. Can't sleep. Thought maybe you'd like some company." He lifted his brows, looking so vulnerable she opened her arms to welcome him.

He swept in and practically lifted her off the floor to kiss her. She responded to him with the depth of emotion circulating throughout her body. He groaned and kicked the front door closed with his foot.

He walked her backwards to her bedroom and lowered her to the bed. He had her undressed in a heartbeat, kissing and touching and smoothing her skin. Within seconds she was ready for him, though he seemed to force himself to slow the pace.

"Let's take our time," he rasped over her neck between warm, wet kisses.

She inhaled, bracketed his face with her hands, and whispered, "Whatever you say…" before drawing him closer for another smoldering kiss.

Just before dawn, Beck withdrew and rolled off Jan then pulled her limp and satisfied body onto his chest. His hand danced down the slope of her spine and came to rest on the silken soft round of her rump. She sighed and cuddled into the crook of his arm and rested her head on his shoulder.

Holding her so naturally brought on a deluge of memories.

"How in the hell did we ever lose track of each other?" he asked.

She lifted her head and glanced lazily at him with hooded eyes, causing a new surge of desire to pulse through his nerves. Before she could answer he broke in.

"It's been eating me up for years. I told you I loved you and I meant it. You said you loved me." She stiffened under his grasp. "What went wrong?"

She swallowed slightly and sat up. A pleading expression, a cut-and-run panic, formed in her eyes. "Beck," she whispered. "I did love you. I meant it when I told you I loved you, but…" She lifted his hand and kissed his fingertips with fevered lips. "Please. Try to understand."

He took hold of her neck and drew her closer to him. "Understand what? That you ran away from me?"

"I didn't run away. My mother sent me."

He ran his hand over her hair, remembering Karen Stewart and the despising stares she was famous for. Don't mess with her daughter's future, her fierce eyes had communicated at every chance. She'd had big plans for January. "I know she hated me, but that never stopped you from sneaking out to see me. You could have gotten a message to me. Somehow."

She covered his mouth with a cold hand. Tears glimmered in her eyes. "Beck, I was pregnant."

He swept her hand away and rose up onto his elbows, a sucker punch stealing his breath. "Pregnant?"

She nodded as tears glistened and flowed over her lids.

"Why didn't you tell me?" He shot up to sitting. "We could have worked something out. I had plans for us."

"You don't understand."

A torrent of mixed-up feelings swept over him—anger, grief, frustration—swirled together, making him feel queasy. He jumped off the bed, fought for balance and set off pacing the floor. "You were pregnant with my child and you didn't tell me?" He bit back the wave of nausea that pressed against his stomach and threatened to move up his throat. "How could you not tell me?"

"I found out the night before you left for bootcamp. Mom threatened to have you arrested for statutory rape if I said anything." She got up, throwing on her robe as she pleaded with him to understand,

"That's horse manure!" He rounded on her and glared, the nausea quickly being replaced with rage. "I had a right to know."

"She told me all kinds of lies to get her way. Made me think she could ruin your military career. She made me promise to go away and lie in order to protect you."

"You should have fought for us, January." He slapped his chest with his palm, trying to keep the wave of rage under control. "You should have told me."

"Beck. Please, try to understand. I did fight for us. The only way I knew how. She wanted me to have an abortion, but I refused."

He stopped in mid-pace. "You didn't have an abortion?"

She shook her head and shuddered with a new wave of tears. "I had the baby."

An eerie cold chill pulsed through him and slid down his spine. "Our baby," he corrected, a bleak hunch strangling the hope that had flickered in his heart.

"I had our baby and gave her up for adoption."

"Without ever telling me?" Red-hot anger surged through him, stamping out the chills.

"I'm sorry," she whimpered, her face going rubbery with emotion.

"Who gave you the right to take my kid and give it away?" He rounded on her. She backed up, fear blooming in her suddenly wide eyes.

"I was young. I didn't know what to do." She gulped for air and shook with emotion. "I didn't want to ruin your life. Please, try to understand."

He grabbed her arms and stared into her watery eyes. She trembled beneath his grasp. "You robbed me of my kid. How could you?"

She crumpled toward the floor. He caught and guided her on her wobbly legs to the bed and helped her sit down. Fury and frustration roared in his chest, drumming a loud rhythm in his temples. He wanted to slam his fist through a wall or yell at the top of his lungs. He wanted to drive his motorcycle a hundred miles an hour to try to outrun the pain that chased him down. She'd given their baby away and never had the courtesy or the courage to utter a word to him about it. This from the girl he'd once trusted with all his heart.

He stared at the woman, the stranger, who only moments before had had him at her mercy when they'd made love like randy teenagers. Never could he have guessed the secret she'd harbored while he'd entered her with the most intimate act of all. She couldn't be trusted. How could she make love to him without telling him?

"How could you?" he roared, after pulling on his jeans and tugging on his sweatshirt. "That girl on the refrigerator. Is that her?"

January gave one nod, rolled toward the bedside table and opened a drawer, from which she produced the framed pictures of the most precious pre-teen he'd ever seen. Remorse took hold as if two huge hands wrapped around his neck and strangled him. He could barely breathe and shook with sorrow as he reached for the frames. He recognized the face, like one of those computer-generated picture versions of two people who wanted to see what their kid would look like. Part January. Part Beck. His daughter. Innocent. Oblivious. Happy.

Unaware he even existed.

"What's her name?" he asked, almost inaudibly.

"Meghan." Her voice quavered. "She's almost thirteen and she lives in northern California with two wonderful people."

"How do you know all that?"

"We had an open adoption. The Williamses had me come and live with them when I was pregnant. That's where I went.

Not modeling school. They helped me finish high school and apply to college. Mom wanted them to pay extra money after the birth, but they tricked her and only agreed to pay it to me when I turned eighteen. I'm a nurse because of them."

He turned a deaf ear to the pleading in her voice. Venomous anger snaked through his veins. He couldn't hold back the raging thoughts. "All for the low price of our baby."

She gasped at the insult he'd lobbed at her. "Please, try to understand…"

"What's to understand? You lied to me and gave my baby away." He wanted to shake sense into her, but didn't dare go near her for fear of what he might do. As a boy, he'd been at the wrong end of the destructive side of rage more often than he wanted to remember. He'd never lift a finger to harm a woman, but his reeling emotions made him doubt his restraint at the moment. He took a step back. "I tried everything to track you down and when you finally called me you acted as if I was nothing to you. Do you remember that?"

She nodded. Apprehension formed like a mask on her face, paralyzing it. She spoke in a drone, staring at the floor. "My mother made me promise to break up with you. You have no idea how much it hurt me to lie to you."

"You made it seem so easy. 'I don't love you any more, Beck. I'm sorry.'" He took his time repeating the words and glared at her. She didn't look back. "Do you remember that? That's exactly what you said." The searing pain he'd felt all those years ago returned as if she'd just broken his heart all over again.

She covered her face with her hands and rocked on her knees on the bed.

"I was young and stupid and scared," she bit out, tears and mucus streaming down her face. "I made a huge mistake, and I've paid for it every day of my life since."

No wonder she'd dreaded seeing him again. No wonder she'd avoided him. No wonder she'd lost the sparkle. She'd traded it in for deceit and guilt, and it had taken a toll on her both physically and mentally.

And she deserved it!

Yet she'd seemed to come back to life in his arms the last couple of days. And he couldn't deny she was a caring and talented nurse. He chewed on the inside of his mouth as he glanced at the picture of his daughter again. The decent side of him wanted to try to understand her plight. But a fierce new wave of anger commandeered his thinking.

"What about me?" He was a father and he'd never even known it. She'd robbed him of what was his, and she could never be trusted again.

Anger flamed in her eyes as she showed the first sign of fighting spirit. "You? You went off to see the world on your big adventure." Her trembling hands splayed across her breasts. "I was just the girl you left behind."

CHAPTER SEVEN

JAN watched a muscle pull in Beck's jaw and clenched her fists, letting her own anger at how unjust he was being fill her, trying her best to keep from falling apart.

"I'm leaving for Afghanistan the end of this month," he said in a guttural tone, changing from outraged to sullen. "Then I'll be out of your life for good." Without saying another word, he left, taking one of the framed pictures of Meghan with him and slamming the door.

Jan stood shivering, afraid to move for fear of stumbling. Tears streamed down her face, and her throat thickened to where she couldn't swallow. She gasped for air, demanding that her mind step in and figure something out while her body went into total meltdown.

She owed it to Beck to make things right, but how could she do that? She'd been in his arms and made love with him and allowed herself to remember every secret thought she'd hoarded for thirteen years. He'd touched her deepest feelings and brought back every memory of what it had been like when they'd been together. Though their bond had remained buried, it was unbroken. She couldn't lose him again.

But was she willing to make a third casualty of Meghan in the process?

Her mind leapt from thought to thought and back again. Nothing made sense. Exhausted from worry, she almost gave up. She could never respect herself until she made things right. Then one last idea popped into her head.

She'd promised the Williamses she'd never interfere with their lives...unless invited. As of today, she promised herself there would be no more lies, and it was time to talk to Yvonne.

The latest letter came into her mind. Meghan was studying genetics and had broached the subject of her adoption. It wasn't like she didn't know she was adopted, it was just that she considered her adoptive parents to be her only parents. The Williamses were reasonable people—maybe they'd understand Beck's need to meet his daughter. But would she jeopardize her relationship with them for lying, and would they forgive her?

And could she guarantee that meeting his child was all Beck wanted? In this litigious age could she trust Beck not to do something horrendous and damaging to everyone involved?

The endless questions whirled in her head. Dear God, she'd botched things up.

Jan knew what she'd done to Beck. She couldn't blame him if he wanted to get Meghan back, prayed he wouldn't try, but couldn't completely trust him either. Regardless, she needed to make it up to him somehow. In order to respect herself and move on with her life, she needed to do something to regain some portion of his respect.

She dropped to her knees with a thud and clutched her

hands together, praying there could be a civilized way out
of this mess. The mess she'd created with her lie.

Grateful that Beck was nowhere in sight, Jan started her
work shift on Monday afternoon. Her stomach had been
in a knot and she'd been unable to eat or sleep. The dark
circles under her eyes had shocked her when she'd washed
her face that morning. Fortunately her glasses covered up
the swelling and bags. Now if she could only find a way
to act as if her entire life hadn't crumbled…again.

She grabbed a chart and walked to the waiting room,
calling out a name. "Jared Winslow?"

Two young men in baggy clothes stood to accompany
a third male dressed similarly into the ward. He hobbled
along, a tight grimace etched deeply on his face. He
moaned with each attempted step. "This is tore up from the
floor up," he uttered between clenched teeth.

Jan searched for a wheelchair and had the friends put
the patient in it. He moaned again.

"What's going on?" she asked.

"Breakdancing," one of them spoke up. "Twitch is a
B-boy. He did a flip that went bad."

"My bad," Jared "Twitch" said.

Jan recalled a range of injuries that had presented in the
ER over the past few years from the athletic, unpredictable
and sometimes dangerous form of dance. The ER staff had
even started naming specific diagnoses to injuries caused
by breakdancing. "Breaker's Neck," "Breakdance Back,"
"Breaker's Thumb," "Brokeback Breaker."

The patient wore a red beret. Jan lifted it from his head
and noticed an area of alopecia. "Twitch" obviously liked

to spin on his head, too. If that was the case, head and neck injuries would need to be ruled out.

"Did you land on your head?"

The gangly trio shook their heads.

"Are you having any numbness or tingling anywhere?" she asked as she wheeled him into the exam room.

The patient tentatively rolled his ankles and wrists. "I can't feel my left foot all the way, and my neck is jacked up."

She thought back to a recent patient with a C5 compression fracture and subluxation who had become a quadriplegic after a botched breakdance front flip where he'd landed on his head. The laminectomy surgery had been unsuccessful. At least Jared's injury was less extreme.

Passing the nurses' station, Jan mentioned to Carmen that her patient would need a thorough neuro examination. For safety's sake, she put a C-collar on "Twitch" and placed him in a supine position on the gurney. If he'd been brought in by EMTs he would have been strapped to a backboard, too.

Expecting to see just Gavin show up, a burst of fireflies winged through her chest when Beck appeared at the bedside with him. She'd just finished taking Jared's vitals, and she fumbled to fold the blood-pressure cuff. She slanted a glance his way and caught him watching her. The stone-cold stare clearly communicated his loathing, and it knocked the breath out of her.

She had to get away.

"Call me if you need anything," she said to Gavin, starting for the door. Thankfully, Gavin had been oblivious to her odd behaviour, concentrating solely on the patient. Before she left, she heard Gavin switch into teacher mode after introducing himself to the patient.

"One time we had a breakdancing injury where a kid flopped when he meant to flip and he had a C7 spinous process fracture."

When Gavin continued on with technical language, she knew his spiel was meant for Beck, not the patient.

"Fortunately," he continued, "there wasn't any neurological deficit. All the kid had to do was wear a soft cervical collar for a few weeks, wait for the swelling to go down, and he was fine. Hopefully, the same will happen for you, Jared. Let's get some stat portable cervical spine films." He called over his shoulder. "Beck, you can do the neuro check."

"I'll order the X-rays now," Jan muttered as she slipped out of the room, devising a plan to avoid Beck for the rest of the shift.

The next morning, Jan's hand trembled as she punched in the numbers she'd only dialed a handful of times in thirteen years. She sat stiffly on the edge of her couch and listened to the phone ring. She'd called during school hours to avoid having Meghan answer the phone.

How would she explain her predicament? She'd always suspected the Williamses knew she'd lied when she'd told them—as her mother had coached her to do—that she didn't know who the father of her baby was. She'd cringed, assuming they'd think much less of her with the implications of that statement, and had worried they might call off the adoption process.

But they'd understood. She hoped they'd understand this time, too.

Yvonne answered the phone with a friendly chirp.

"Hello. This is January Stewart-Ashworth."

"January, what a pleasant surprise. How can I help you?"

She repeated her story as she'd rehearsed a good hour before getting up the nerve to make the call. When she'd finished, there was dead silence on the other end.

After a pause, Yvonne responded with a cautious tone. "Do you anticipate any problems from this Beck Braxton person? Do we need to get a lawyer involved?"

"I don't believe so, Mrs. Williams. I believe he's a reasonable man. He's a SWAT officer and a Special Forces trained medic in the National Guard. He doesn't have the time or the inclination to make a big stink out of this, I don't think."

"Let me talk to Daryl and I'll get back to you. I have to admit, it would be the perfect time for this. Meggie has a whole list of questions for her birth parents to answer for a term paper on genetics. Of course, Daryl and I couldn't answer the questions. We were going to e-mail them to you." After another pause, she said, "Maybe this is a blessing in disguise. This genetics-genealogy business has opened a whole can of worms. Lately, she's been very curious about her birth parents."

They ended the call on a friendly note, and Jan cautiously allowed herself to feel hopeful that things might work out. She understood that she'd never have a chance to be friends with Beck again, and it tore a chunk out of her heart. But she'd violated that privilege when she'd allowed her mother to pressure her into lying thirteen years ago. If this was the price she'd have to pay for her deceit, she'd have to accept it and move on. It was finally time to come out of hiding and reclaim her self-respect.

Her insides roiled with the thought of losing Beck again. In the short time they'd had together since he'd come to

Mercy Hospital, the emotionally comatose part of her had started to come back to life. His touch had resurrected feelings she'd shoved into the depths of her soul, and the intense love she'd once had for him felt as if it had never died. How could that be?

She shook her head and blinked back the sharp pin-pricks behind her lids. She hadn't cried this much since she'd first been pregnant.

Panic struck through her core. Once she heard back from Yvonne, one way or the other, she'd have to confront the man she'd betrayed—the man who wanted nothing more to do with her. Beck.

The thought sent her stomach reeling, and she had to rush for the bathroom.

Later, with every ounce of courage she could muster, Jan stood at Beck's front door and prepared to knock. What she had to say needed to be said in person. She couldn't change the past, but she sure as hell would never repeat it. Even if it was already too late, she'd never lie to Beck again.

Did that include telling him how she still felt about him?

She'd called Carmen and gotten Beck's address then looked up the directions to his Glendale home on the Internet. She hadn't dared warn him she was coming for fear he wouldn't talk to her.

The door opened after one knock. If she trusted her people-reading skills, he wasn't the least bit happy to see her.

"What are you doing here?" he rasped. She heard the low sounds of a TV on in the background.

"We need to talk," she said, aware her voice sounded thin and stringy.

"We said everything we needed to say the other day."

"We need to talk about our daughter."

His expression went still. She could see the closed steel trap of resistance open just a little. "What do you mean?"

"May I come in?"

He slanted a tentative glance over his shoulder. A chill rolled down her spine. Had he already replaced her with another woman? Had she been a fool to think—to dream—that she might still have meant something to him?

Without another word, he stepped aside and motioned for her to come in. All of the insecure images vanished.

She entered his modest California bungalow with trepidation. It felt cool inside and he'd kept the house dark by leaving the curtains closed, though it was already noon. Large painted canvases covered his walls. Landscapes with colorful broad strokes, detailed abstract portraits, and intricate designs with whimsical patterns, all of them had the mark of Beck.

"Did you paint these?"

He nodded, without elaborating.

"They're beautiful," she said, feeling waylaid and a bit like Alice in Wonderland. Her little painted egg was just the tip of his talent. Thankfully, he'd pursued his natural gift, and she knew she'd played a role in the discovery.

He'd obviously worked all night, and appeared sleepy and somewhat disheveled. Dark stubble outlined his jaw, and the shirt he wore was unbuttoned and wrinkled, as though he'd slept in his clothes. Had he been suffering as much as she had?

He switched off the television. "I've made some coffee—want a cup?"

To be polite, and hopefully to ease the situation in any way she could, she nodded. "Thanks."

He pointed to a streamlined honey-colored leather couch. "Have a seat. I'll be right back."

So far there'd been no sign of the furious man from a few nights ago. She sat primly on the edge of the couch and hoped and prayed they'd be able to work civilly through their situation.

Shortly, he handed her a warm cup and barely caught her eyes before looking away. Taking his own mug, he sat on the opposite end of the couch. "So what do we do now?"

Jan stopped in mid-sip and swallowed with difficulty. She cleared her throat while her stomach protested. "Well, I've made a phone call to the Williamses. They're Meghan's parents, and they've agreed to meet with us."

He sat straighter. "What makes you think I want to meet her?"

"I know you, Beck."

His eyes drifted toward her face after nearly burning a hole in the ceiling. "I used to think I knew you, too." He looked away, his gaze shifting around the room. A familiar expression of caution returned. "Why does she want to meet us?"

"Meghan has a school project she needs us to help her with."

"Wait. Wait. She's going to meet her birth parents and all she wants to do is interview us?" Pain and disbelief registered in his eyes. "We could do that online."

Jan ached with every word she needed to say. "We're strangers to her, Beck. Her mom and dad are the only parents she knows. I suspect we're a mere curiosity. But she's interested and they're willing."

Muscles twitched at both sides of his jaw. "So I'm just a 'mere curiosity' to my own daughter." He shook his head, disgust oozing from his expression. He rubbed his hand over his head. "I wouldn't be surprised if she hated me."

Tension filled her throat along with a wave of nausea and sadness. She couldn't take another sip of coffee and placed the cup on the nearby glass tabletop. "No more than she would hate me."

They co-ordinated with the Williamses and agreed to meet in Sacramento Capitol Park on Saturday afternoon. Sacramento being 360 miles away, Beck and January agreed to drive up together the day before.

Expecting nothing more than a honk of the horn to alert her of his arrival early on Friday morning, Jan was surprised when Beck knocked on her door. She'd been ready and had sat chewing what was left of her fingernails while waiting for him with an overnight bag on her lap.

How in the world would she spend seven hours cooped up in a car with Beck, the man who hated her?

At the sound of his knock she leapt off the couch, almost crying out in surprise. Before opening the door, she composed herself and ran quick fingers through her hair. Did it matter how she looked?

Beck stood on the other side of her screen, appearing serious, and seriously handsome. From the look and smell of him he was fresh out of the shower, with smooth-shaven cheeks and tantalizing aftershave. He wore snug-fitting jeans and a cornflower-blue polo shirt, which highlighted his firm arms and broad shoulders and made his hazel eyes dark and mysterious. She quickly glanced away.

"Hi," she muttered.

"You ready?"

She held up her overnight bag in answer.

"Then let's go." He held the screen door open for her while she locked up, stepping aside so as not to make any contact with her, then allowed her to lead the way to his car. He zipped around her in time to open the door and wait for her to slip inside.

The distinctive aroma of fresh-brewed coffee surprised her.

When Beck got into the car and started the engine he casually mentioned that he'd bought them both some coffee and a croissant. Even in his anger he was considerate, and that made a dull ache begin in her gut.

"Thanks," she muttered, before taking a sip and noticing he hadn't forgotten the cream she liked. Somehow she managed to break off a piece of apple-filled croissant, but it tasted bland in comparison to the great smell.

They drove in agonizing silence, his talking GPS system the only sound. When she'd finished her croissant and coffee, she thanked him again and offered to put his empty cup and pastry sack in the car's trash bag. He nodded his thanks, and slanted a look at her. His gaze lighted briefly on her face then flew back to the road. From the corner of her eye she watched the muscle in his jaw twitch. The poor man had probably been grinding his teeth to a pulp lately. If she could only read his mind.

To break the monotonous silence, Beck turned on the radio and found a station that brought back memories from their high-school days. He quickly switched the station to a light jazz one.

Jan gazed out the window at the dry brown hills surrounding the northbound freeway. This would be the longest drive of her life.

Two hours into the trip, in the middle of nowhere, he pulled off the road at a rest stop so they could use the facilities and stretch their legs. When she left the ladies' room she saw Beck across the courtyard talking on his cellphone. A wave of melancholy caught her by surprise. Who was he talking to? She had no clue about his personal life, or who his friends were.

She'd heard through Carmen that he'd kept vigil at his partner's bedside while he'd been in hospital, instead of working in the ER. That sounded like the Beck she knew. She glanced back at Beck on the phone. For all she knew, he could be talking to a lawyer.

He flipped the phone closed just as he noticed Jan approaching him. "All set?" he asked, sounding almost affable.

"Yes." She forced a smile. His gaze met hers and for half a second he looked directly into her eyes. If she could only interpret his expression, maybe she could find a way to make him understand why she'd given their daughter away rather than tell him she was pregnant. Maybe she could force him to see she'd done it to protect him and make his life better. If only. But sooner than she could think of one word to say, he'd started toward the car.

They barely said another word until they were halfway between Los Angeles and Sacramento. "What do you say we stop in Fresno for lunch?"

Not the least bit hungry, she agreed to it to break the tortured silence. They decided on a sit-down lunch of barbecue chicken sandwiches and cold lemonade at a roadside diner. Each bite felt like a golfball to swallow. Again she noticed him studying her, and wished she could hear his thoughts, though she feared what they might be. Did everything taste like cardboard to him, too?

"How's this going to work?" he asked.

She pulled out of deep contemplation. "What do you mean?"

"We're just going to show up in a park and meet our kid and act as if it's completely normal?"

Jan managed to swallow the lump of bread and chicken before answering. "For Meghan's sake, we'll have to."

He shook his head and stared at the table. Jan couldn't force another bite. The bitter tang of the lemonade almost brought tears to her eyes, but she knew their circumstances didn't help.

At 4:30 p.m. they arrived at their downtown Sacramento hotel, having said fewer than a hundred words to each other the whole day. Before parting ways for their individual rooms, they agreed to meet at nine the next morning for the short drive to the gardens at Capitol Park.

Jan couldn't stop herself from watching Beck's long strides and tight butt as he walked away. The ever-present attraction humming through her body didn't seem to wane, regardless of how screwed up their personal relationship was. He'd told her just a few short days ago that she still took his breath away. They'd made love as if they'd never been apart, yet now they were acting like complete strangers. Strangers with a daughter.

By seven, Jan couldn't spend one more minute in her room, watching vapid game shows on TV. Needing fresh air, she opted to eat al fresco rather than order room service. She combed her hair, touched up her make-up and changed her top to the bright pink blouse she intended to wear the next day, then set out, making sure she'd brought her room card.

The moment she arrived at the quiet dining patio, she wanted to turn back. There, at a table in the corner, sat Beck by himself, ordering from a waiter. She wanted to hide behind the potted ficus plant, but before she could make her get-away, he noticed her and waved her over. Obviously, he was being polite. She took a deep breath and approached the wrought-iron and glass-topped table. He motioned for the waiter to leave the menu.

"I'm having a beer. Would you like something to drink?"

Oh, what the heck. Maybe it would make their agonizing awkwardness a wee bit better. "I'll have a glass of Zinfandel," she said to the waiter.

She glanced back and noticed Beck's eyes traveling over her. Immediate warmth started at her neck and tiptoed up her cheeks. To her disbelief, he smiled at her. Out of reflex, she smiled tentatively back.

"So what do we do now?" he asked, elbows on the table, one hand fisted inside the other.

"Beats me."

"Maybe we should come up with a game plan. You know, in case Meghan wants to know why we gave her away."

"The Williamses have told her I was a teenage mother. So we can say that you were in the service and got sent away. That's basically the truth."

"I want to make sure she understands that I didn't know about her until now."

The request sent a boulder to her stomach. "OK." Jan

closed her eyes and chewed on her upper lip, reeling from yet more consequences from her misguided decision years before. "If that's what you want."

He nodded, his eyes sure and unwavering.

The waiter brought their drinks and Jan had an urge to gulp the entire glass down to help relieve the pain stabbing her heart, but she sipped as if she wasn't wounded and her world hadn't suddenly been knocked sideways.

One fact was true. Living a lie would always catch up with you, and that day of judgment was staring her down and daring her to try to break free.

The restaurant, with all the noise and clatter, went suddenly quiet. Beck had concentrated so thoroughly on January's response that every other sound had been tuned out. It reminded him of listening to noisy frogs in springtime when, as if on cue, they'd all stop simultaneously. That silence often seemed louder than the chorus of croaking.

He'd been totally out of control of this situation. Now he planned to take back the reins. His daughter needed to know he hadn't allowed her to be given away. If only he'd known, things would have been different. He'd contacted a lawyer to figure out his rights. He didn't want to disrupt the girl's life, but he wanted to be free to visit her—on his own if possible. He needed to make sure the Williamses couldn't put a restraining order on him if he persisted.

When he'd called his mother earlier in the day, she'd reminded him about the serenity prayer, the prayer she prayed daily as the wife of an alcoholic. She repeated the part that made the most sense to Beck's situation. "Grant me the serenity to accept the things I cannot change."

Beck swigged his beer and watched January shift uncomfortably in the booth. What would he have done if he had known? Even if he'd helped out financially, wouldn't January still have been the one bearing the brunt of parenting responsibility? Hell, she hadn't even been a senior in high school.

So many times today on the drive up he'd tried to ignore the part of him that had wanted to pull off the road and hold January and tell her he understood how difficult it must have been for her. But each time he allowed that line of thought, he reminded himself that she had chosen to keep him in the dark. She deserved whatever fallout came with the lie.

As soon as he met his daughter, and established his own line of communication, he'd stay out of January's life for good and pursue a relationship with Meghan. He could find another woman to have mind-blowing sex with. He'd found them before. No problem.

He took another drink to ward off the chills that spiraled down his spine as he remembered how much more sex meant with January. How holding her in his arms felt so right, as if they were meant to be, and how no other woman in his life had ever come close to giving him that feeling.

Nah, he couldn't go down that path. She needed to pay for her mistakes. He couldn't give in to the desire vibrating through every fiber in his body to hold and protect her and make things a little bit easier.

And—aw hell—now she was crying.

He scooted his chair closer and handed her his napkin. "What's going on?" He meant to keep up his hard façade, but his voice sounded husky with concern.

She fought off her outburst by shaking her head, dabbing at her eyes and sniffing. "I'm sorry. Just ignore me. It's been a long day, that's all."

Without thinking, his hand shot to her shoulder, patted and massaged. "We'll get through this," he said grudgingly.

"I don't want Meghan to hate you because of me, Beck."

"Look. We'll just have to wait and see how this plays out tomorrow."

The waitress arrived with their meal. Beck didn't move his chair back. Instead, he moved his silverware over, feeling the insistent draw of sympathy even while fighting it.

"Eat your dinner," he said, pretending that their world wasn't about to crash around them tomorrow.

She regained her composure, sniffing and wiping the last of the wetness from her eyes. She stuck out her chin, the way she'd once done when she'd been determined about something, and nodded. "You're right. I can't change things and I definitely can't predict how tomorrow will go." She took another sip of wine and Beck ordered another for her.

"Might as well relax tonight. Get a good night's sleep." He thought about taking a bite of the salmon he'd ordered, but didn't want to remove his hand from her shoulder. He drew her closer and gave her one brief squeeze, then caught himself before he kissed her temple. Breaking free, he announced, "Let's eat."

Holding a grudge seemed harder than it should be. Beck tried his best to pepper their mostly quiet meal with superficial conversation, using the excuse that he couldn't take any more silence. He couldn't help seeing the pain in her eyes as she dutifully answered his queries, and it chipped away at his armor.

When the meal was over, he walked her back to her

hotel room, fighting the urge to take her hand. Why couldn't he just stay mad at her? It would make things so much easier. Because she looked so beaten and vulnerable, and it ripped at his heart.

After she'd fumbled through her purse for the magnetic card and had slid it into the slot, she glanced up at him. Obviously feeling the effects of a glass and a half of wine with her dinner, she studied him with softened blue eyes. "I'd give all the money in the world for things to be different."

He wasn't sure what the hell came over him, but he went with it and leaned forward and brushed her lips with his. Because that wasn't enough—it was never enough with January—he hovered close, listening to her measured breathing, then kissed her again. She stiffened, but when he pressed against her warm, soft mouth, she relaxed and kissed him back. He cupped her shoulders and kept the kiss in the tender range, though already embers of desire were kindling in his core.

Break it off, he told himself as his tongue touched the tip of hers. There was no such thing as a friendly, reassuring kiss with January.

But a little voice way in the back of his head interrupted the pleasure. She'd done a horrible thing. She'd lied to him. For years. She didn't deserve his kindness or trust ever again.

And history couldn't be changed.

Finding it suddenly easy to marshal self-discipline, he ended the kiss. She wasn't the only one willing to give up all the money in the world for their situation to be different.

"Ditto," was all he could say, as he briskly stood up and walked away.

CHAPTER EIGHT

THE next morning January and Beck met in the hotel lobby. She'd eaten a light breakfast in her room, but her jangling nerves had made it almost impossible to digest. She took a deep breath and approached him. He hopped out of the lobby chair, where he'd been reading the newspaper, and gave her a businesslike nod. She pretended her heart wasn't pounding against her breastbone. "Good morning," she said.

"Hey."

She'd called the Williamses and verified the area of Capital Park they'd planned to meet. The rose gardens shouldn't be that hard to find.

With all of her heart, she wanted to turn and run. "Ready?" Could he be feeling the same?

"As ready as I'll ever be." He tossed her a tentative smile and opened the lobby door. He strode toward his car at a quick clip and she had to scuttle to keep up. The passenger door was open and waiting when she arrived.

Anxiety had dried up every drop of saliva and had now started to work on squeezing the air out of her lungs. How must Beck feel?

It took several minutes in the car for her to realize the

sun was out and the temperature was pleasantly warm. When they approached the forty-acre park in the center of the city, her stomach got in on the nervous act. Knots and butter-flies competed for space. When Beck parked and they started to walk toward the lush grass, the first thing she noticed was an over-abundance of squirrels. She swal-lowed the paper-like wad of jangled nerves in her throat, and without further thought reached for Beck's hand.

She couldn't go through with this on her own.

He didn't pull away, but held her hand with warm reas-surance, and though nothing had changed between them, it made her feel a bit more able to face what lay ahead.

Due to her growing skittishness, it was almost impos-sible to appreciate the colorful park with tall palms lining the path. Yet she noticed an incredible assortment of trees including her favorite, magnolia, and used its bold fra-grance as a distraction on the walk across the vast lawn.

When they made their way toward the rose garden, she might have turned and run if it hadn't been for the anchor of Beck's hand. Moisture had developed between their palms, and she couldn't decide if it was due to her anxiety or his.

She took a deep breath and looked up at him. He nodded encouragingly as he tugged her along. Maybe there was a chance to make it through this encounter and still maintain a relationship with Beck after all.

Jan spied the Williamses sitting on a park bench in the middle of the rose garden. Under different circumstances the multitude of colors and overpowering scent of roses would have taken her breath away, but all she focussed on was one little girl.

The herd of butterflies that had gathered in her stomach

burst into flight, sending anxious ripples throughout her body. She squeezed Beck's hand tighter. What was he thinking?

Meghan sat between her adopted parents with eyes the size of half-dollars. She turned her head and said something to her father then quickly looked back as Beck and Jan approached. Pre-teen thin and without a trace of curves, she was dressed in a hooded baby-blue sweatshirt with Asian letters on it, and embroidered denim blue jeans. The sweatshirt was almost the exact color of Beck's polo shirt. Her eyes were set deep, like Beck's, and the light blue contrasted with her full and beautiful long brown hair.

After giving birth and holding her briefly, Jan had handed Meghan into the welcoming arms of her new parents. Since then Jan had only seen pictures of Meghan over the years of her development, and had never ventured to see her again in person for fear of confusing the child. The impact of coming face to face with her birth daughter made Jan's legs falter. Beck switched hands and his newly freed hand shot to the small of her back to steady her.

The blood in Jan's head retreated to her feet, causing the park to swim around the periphery of her vision. No. Not now. She refused to pass out. She stood stick straight and drew in a long breath, determined to get hold of herself. "I'll be OK," she muttered to Beck.

He looked doubtfully into her eyes, but let go as she'd indicated she wanted him to. He remained close by, as though ready to catch her if she fell, and when she gave evidence of being OK by walking a little quicker, he strode ahead and introduced himself to the Williamses.

He reached out and shook hands with both parents, then drawled charmingly, "And you must be Meghan."

"Uh-huh." Her quiet, breathy reply was almost inaudible.

"This is January and I'm Beck. It's a pleasure to finally meet you, young lady."

The girl swallowed. And if it were possible, her eyes grew wider. Still no smile. Beck didn't miss a beat.

"We hear you need some help with your science project."

Meghan blushed and nodded. "Uh-huh."

January reached for Yvonne's hand and shook it in greeting. "It's so good to see you again." Their handshake turned into a tight hug. Daryl stood by, awaiting his turn.

Meghan cautiously watched everything, fiddling with her notebook and curling her brightly polished toes in her flip-flops.

Beck folded his arms, focused solely on the girl. "So what grade are you in?"

"Eighth."

"Fantastic. You like middle school?"

"I guess."

"Oh, come on, you're a great student," her mother broke in.

Meghan flashed a typical impatient pre-teen glare at Yvonne, quickly followed by another blush.

After a long silence, while Meghan glanced back and forth between Jan and Beck, she finally said in a quavering voice, "Are you guys really my birth parents?"

Jan looked at Beck, and was nearly knocked over by the angst on his face. Like the trouper he was, he tried to remain cheery, and Jan suspected only Meghan might be oblivious to his pain. Surely Daryl and Yvonne could read the deep sadness behind his guarded expression.

"We are," he said in a strong and steady voice.

"Are you guys married?"

"No," they said in unison, glancing at each other awkwardly.

"You look so young," Meghan said.

Daryl and Yvonne had been in their late thirties when they'd adopted Meghan, and were now well into middle age. Compared to Jan and Beck, of course, they'd seem old to a pre-teen. Weren't all parents "old" to teenagers?

"We were. Let that be a lesson to you about having sex as a teenager," Beck said, then quickly glanced at Daryl and Yvonne as though making sure that topic was OK.

"Don't worry," Daryl said, "we've already started talking about that. We have a very open relationship."

Beck nodded. "Good. You don't want to end up like us. I'd just turned eighteen and had joined the military, and January was only in the eleventh grade." Beck edged his way next to Meghan on the bench. "We were too young to be parents. I hope you can understand that."

Meghan looked at her feet. "My old babysitter is pregnant. She's seventeen." She glanced up at Jan. "She's keeping it."

Finally, Jan found her voice. "It will be very hard for her, but I'm glad she's going to keep the baby. If that's what she wants." She worried how that might sound, and decided to clarify what she'd meant.

Jan knelt in front of Meghan and took one of her hands. It felt fragile and tiny. "Meghan, if I had thought I could be a good parent for you, I would have done anything to keep you. Beck had just left for the military and never even knew. Then I met your future parents and knew immediately that they were the most perfect people in the world for you. I didn't give you up for adoption because I didn't love you. I did it because I loved you with all my heart, and I knew it would be the best thing."

Jan couldn't stop tears forming in her eyes. Meghan's eyes did the same. "I have to help my babysitter balance her checkbook. And sometimes she forgets lots of stuff. Maybe she is too young." Meghan made her first attempt at a smile, with noticeable blue colored braces. Was she trying to soothe Jan's pain?

When Jan glanced at Beck, his eyes were watering, too.

He touched her hand briefly, and cleared his throat. "So I hear you've got a bunch of questions for us."

Meghan nodded. "Yeah."

"Well, let's get started, then," he said, making a great play at keeping things casual and on a lighter note by changing the topic.

An hour and twenty pages of notes later in decidedly plump and diagonal cursive, Meghan and her parents thanked both Beck and Jan profusely and prepared to leave. There was no offer to join them for lunch, or to stop by the Williamses' home before they left town. They'd obviously decided to keep this a practical meeting, nothing more.

And Jan respected their decision.

Beck reached out to hug Meghan and she graced him with a few seconds of a half-hearted squeeze. Jan gave her a quick cuddle and kissed the top of Meghan's sweet-smelling head. She took a deep breath to help remember the fragrance mixed with the roses. The Williamses also hugged both of them…and then they left.

Beck and Jan stood watching.

Halfway across the rose garden, Meghan turned back

toward them and waved goodbye. Jan couldn't hold in the torment another moment. As she waved and smiled encouragingly, hot tears streamed down her cheeks. She dared to look at Beck. Pain contorted his face as he fought to keep his composure. His mouth formed a thin line of tension, his brows pulled tightly together, and huge teardrops flowed out of his large hazel eyes. His nostrils flared as he struggled to keep from bawling. With hands tightly fisted and balanced on his hips, he looked like a man withstanding torture.

Jan wanted to drop to her knees and beg his forgiveness. If only she could turn back time and fix all her mistakes. She wished she could erase this moment and start fresh, free of guilt and pain, because she couldn't stand the burden another second. But there stood Beck, reminding her how callous and cruel she'd been. She'd thought only of herself, never giving him an ounce of consideration.

And now she'd done the emotional equivalent of tearing him limb from limb.

Swallowing back tears, she said, "Please, forgive me, Beck."

He shook his head and gave her a tormented glance before pinching the bridge of his nose. He recovered his composure and stared at the sky briefly, but still didn't utter a sound.

The pain in his eyes sent Jan over the edge. Her body protested, bile rose up her throat, and suddenly she needed to run for the bushes to heave.

In the midst of waves of nausea, with heat rolling across her skin one second and chills the next, she felt a warm palm at the center of her back, then another hand cupping her shoulder.

Beck.

He lifted her out of the bushes and helped her stand. Somewhere he'd found some tissues and handed them to her. She wanted to throw herself at his feet and beg for mercy, but couldn't move. She felt wretched and undeserving of his charity, and slapped at his hand, then thanked him with a defeated nod as she accepted the tissues.

"Let's go back to the hotel," he said hoarsely.

And without another word, she followed.

If Beck clamped his jaw any tighter, it would snap. He utilized every interrogation technique he'd ever learned to disguise the depth of his anguish. January was hurting as much as he was, he could read it all over her. He didn't need to add to her already overwhelming guilt.

If January had only been honest and told him he was going to be a father, he would have made sure she'd waited for him. He would have married her and brought her to the military base to live. They could have been a family instead of three strangers.

Of course, they would have had to live on a soldier's pay and she would have had to drop out of high school. And the responsibility of a baby would have tested their characters like nothing else in life, at a time when other kids their age would have been partying in college.

His foot pressed heavily on the gas pedal in the car and once he realized how fast he was driving he forced himself to slow down. January stared out the window, occasionally dabbing at her eyes and nose with another tissue he'd produced from his glove compartment.

Wanting with all of his might to blame her for botching up the decision to give their daughter away, he couldn't quite give in to sanctimony. He'd knocked her up and taken off. Her mother had exploited the situation with threats of having him arrested.

January had once said she loved him more than anything in the world. Maybe she'd told him the truth, and adoption had been her way of protecting him and the baby. Maybe it had been the noblest gesture a young and frightened girl could have made.

Nah, he wasn't going to let January off the hook that easily.

He wanted to strangle Karen Stewart for manipulating January, but the final decision had come down to her and her alone, and, what the hell, none of it mattered any more. His flesh and blood knew two other people as parents, and he'd been relegated to being some stranger to play Twenty Questions with.

He bashed the horn with his palm when a driver cut him off. January sat up straight, on alert. Tightening his lips, he shook his head. "I'm sorry. That guy ticked me off."

He didn't dare look into her eyes. The sorrow and guilt he'd seen there all morning nearly drove him out of his mind. He needed to take her home. Then he needed to stay as far away from her as he could for the rest of his life.

They were packed, had checked out, and were ready to drive home when Jan's cellphone rang. It was Daryl Williams.

"Are you guys still in town? Meghan has just had a freak accident. Yvonne hates the sight of blood and I'm not sure if she needs stitches or not. The thing is, our doctor's office is closed on Saturdays, and we called the local ER. They said it would be a three-hour wait just to be seen. I was wondering, since you folks are medical people, if there was any chance you could take a look at her knee? I'll explain more when you get here."

"Of course," she said. "Where do you live?"

Ten minutes later Jan and Beck parked in the driveway of the Williamses' suburban home. Yvonne came rushing out the door, her face tense with concern.

"I've got her leg all wrapped up. I think the bleeding has stopped. Come inside."

Beck picked up the medical kit he always kept in his car and Jan led the way. Once inside, they found Meghan lying on a sheet on top of the couch. She looked pale compared to her healthy color from earlier in the day. She sheepishly eyed Jan and Beck as they entered the living room.

Daryl paced, poised to jump the moment Beck and Jan entered. "OK. We're going to be perfectly honest here. Once we got home, Meghan took off."

"Dad," Meghan broke in.

"Sweetie, I'm going to be honest with them. Yvonne and I spent an hour looking for her. We found her in her favorite thinking tree at the local park. She knows better than to climb up there. We used to scold her all the time, but that's beside the point." He rambled on about all the circumstances leading up to Meghan's injury. "She didn't want to talk to us, so I climbed up after her. She tried to get away and almost fell. I grabbed her just in time, but her knee caught a small branch. She hit it real hard. Got cut pretty deep." He sighed and shook his head. He looked at his daughter, concern on his face. "Does it still hurt, Meggie?"

Meghan shook her head. "Maybe just a little."

Jan sat on the edge of the sofa. "May I take a look?" she asked. Meghan nodded.

Carefully unwrapping the makeshift bandage, Jan noticed there wasn't nearly as much blood as she'd expected from Daryl's frantic call. Peeling away the last of the wrap she saw a half-moon-shaped laceration on Meghan's knee. The top skin flap had been pushed back and she was pretty sure she could see a portion of the pale white patella.

Jan glanced up into Meghan's anxious eyes. "I'm afraid you do need stitches. It's a deep cut."

Beck moved in. "Let me have a look." He nodded. "Yep. She's right." He winked at Meghan. "Piece of cake. You want me to fix it?"

Meghan chewed on her lower lip, and tentatively nodded.

"No problem," Beck said. He fished through his bag for a suture kit, then Jan and Beck went to the kitchen to wash their hands.

"Has Meghan had a tetanus shot recently?" Jan called out.

"Last year," came Yvonne's reply.

Back at the couch, Jan thoroughly cleaned the wound with soap and water and then antiseptic solution. She patted Meghan's hand. "You'll need to keep this area clean and dry for a few days and you'll have to keep your leg straight for a day or two. Then it will be stiff for a few days after that. Just take it easy." She drew up the local anesthetic. "I don't know how you feel about needles, but this tiny little pinprick will hurt a lot less than having stitches without it." She smiled empathetically at the girl. "Are you OK with that?"

Meghan hesitated, but nodded, not making a peep. She held her mother's hand and squeezed until her knuckles were white as Jan injected local anesthetic. When she'd finished, she switched places with Beck, who began carefully suturing the wound.

Meghan's shoulders tensed and rose. Her mother rubbed them. Jan decided to help distract her.

"You'll need to keep these stitches in for a week. Yvonne, you can remove them by snipping the sutures with small scissors and pulling them out with tweezers, or if you prefer…" Jan babbled on almost as nervous as she assumed Meghan was. She made eye contact with her, and the girl appeared to be listening intently in order to ignore the stitches. Since she had a captive audience, she continued. "If the skin gets red, tender to touch, or starts making pus, you'll need to see a doctor. But if you keep it covered and clean for the first few days, though it was a dirty wound, it may not be a problem." Jan kept chattering on. "You can use an ice pack on and off for the local swelling for the next couple of days if you want." Looking at Yvonne, she said, "Just don't leave the sutures in over a week."

Before everyone realized it, Beck had completed eight stitches, perfectly aligned in a half-circle. He patted Meghan's calf. "Whenever you look at this scar, I want you to think of me, OK?" He gave his signature-charming smile.

Meghan blushed, rolled her eyes and said, "OK."

"Hey," Daryl said. "We can't thank you two enough. Won't you stay for dinner?"

Jan glanced at Beck. He subtly shook his head.

"We'd love to, but we have a really long drive home and we both have to work tomorrow," she said, wishing with all her heart that they could stay and get to know their daughter a bit more.

"Tell you what," Beck said, bending down and lifting Meghan up into his arms. "I'll carry you to your room so you can take a nap."

Yvonne led the way, and Jan followed them down the hall, last in line of the double parent parade. She already knew how deeply these wonderful people loved Meghan, but seeing her bedroom cinched how well they cared for her. Meghan wanted for nothing. Maybe she was a bit spoiled, but surely the child knew she was loved.

Beck glanced around the room and grinned. "Gee. How many shades of pink are there?"

Meghan clucked her tongue and rolled her eyes again, then fought off a contented smile. Beck slanted a glance at Jan, as if the pink room was more evidence that Meghan was indeed her daughter.

They both noticed a couple of paintings on the wall at the same time. One was of a horse and the other was a fairly decent attempt at a self-portrait.

"Did you paint those?" Beck asked.

Meghan nodded shyly.

"They're really good. You know, I do some painting myself," he said.

"Really?"

He nodded at her with a pleased smile. "Really."

"Maybe some time I can see them?"

"Maybe."

As they prepared to leave, the girl's timid, sweet voice stopped them. "Thank you for everything. I was mad at first, but now I think maybe you guys did the right thing."

Jan glanced at Beck, who stood perfectly still, staring at the daughter who looked incredibly like him. She'd as much as told them it was OK that they'd given her up. Would it be enough?

It would have to be. "Thank you," Jan said, as she returned to the frilly bed, bent and kissed her birth daughter on the forehead. "That means so much to me."

Beck wasn't far behind, waiting his turn to kiss her cheek. "Is it OK if I write to you guys?"

Both Jan and Beck looked toward her parents before answering. Daryl gave a nod. Tears brimmed in Yvonne's eyes, but she gave her OK, too.

"You know what?" Beck thumbed her chin. "I'd really like that. And I'll write back to you."

After exchanging addresses, without saying another word, they shook hands with the Williamses one last time, waved goodbye to Meghan and left for Los Angeles.

On the long drive home, Jan had plenty of time to think. She'd screwed up Beck's life, but he'd handled today like a true gentleman. For a guy who'd been defiant his whole life, he'd channeled that energy into military precision and upholding the law, and had turned into one incredible human being. Too bad she'd royally messed things up between them with her lies, because it would be impossible to find another guy anywhere near as perfect for her as Beck.

When they arrived home that night, having promised herself never to lie to Beck again, Jan stared into his deep almond-shaped eyes when he walked her to the door. She still had feelings for him. Should she tell him?

He pulled her into a hug and she relaxed against his firm chest and shoulder.

"What a day." He exhaled.

"Yeah. Thank you for being there for me." The warmth of his embrace lulled her. She inhaled his distinct scent, marveling how she could probably pick him out of a crowd blindfolded.

"I know how hard it was for you," he whispered into her ear.

He understood.

She sucked in a relieved breath, wanting to kiss him with gratitude and maybe ask him inside. She lifted her cheek from his shoulder to find his mouth.

He spoke before she had a chance to kiss him. "Just as hard as it is for me to tell you that I've decided it's best if we don't see each other any more."

CHAPTER NINE

JAN couldn't argue against Beck's decision. She'd marched him through hell and back by lying to him and had cheated him of knowing his daughter. How could she expect him to forgive and forget? Even if he did admit to their obvious and growing attraction to each other, their adopted child would stand in the way of him trusting her. Meghan would be a symbol of how Jan had betrayed him.

She'd always thought that love was worth fighting for, but without spending more time with Beck she couldn't know for sure if the feelings blossoming in her heart were, in fact, true love. There were so many appealing qualities about him to sweep her away. It could just be exceptionally hot lust, but deep down she didn't think so. Even if it was love, he'd be leaving again soon. They just weren't meant to be.

Anyway, none of it mattered because Beck had ended everything. He never wanted to see her again, and, tough as it seemed, she'd just have to get over it.

She deserved no better.

One week later, true to his word, Jan still hadn't crossed paths with Beck at the hospital.

There had been a big rigmarole over the SWAT shootout at the bank. For the following two weeks after the attempted armed robbery the evening news featured the story every night. The loss of one innocent life had been blamed on the LAPD instead of the bank robbers for instigating the whole situation. The police department hadn't protected the bystanders enough when they'd swarmed the bank to rescue the hostages, or so they'd been accused. Even the families of the deceased bank robbers had lawyers working on their behalf, claiming unlawful loss of life. One lawyer claimed they'd allowed his client to bleed to death while attending to the uninjured hostages.

A whisper of hope made Jan wish that was the reason Beck hadn't been around. That his absence had only been business related, not because of her.

The world seemed crazily out of order, but no more than Jan's personal life. When she was completely honest with herself, a life without Beck, the man she'd come to realize she still loved, seemed sadly lacking.

Carmen knew something was up, and in her usual unsubtle way insisted on discussing it with Jan in the nurses' station.

"Are you and that medic hunk, Beck, still seeing each other?" At least she'd lowered her voice.

Jan snorted her reply. "He doesn't want to ever see me again."

"I thought something was up. What went wrong?"

Jan gave Carmen a defeated stare. "What didn't go wrong?"

"Are you avoiding him?"

"He's avoiding me."

"Then take this chart and bring this patient into room one, because I just saw him head for the locker room."

Wide-eyed and edgy, Jan rushed toward the waiting area, hoping she could get her patient into the exam room before Beck came back to the ED.

With her concentration shot, she called the next patient's name and after one glance left all thoughts of Beck behind. Another teenager and what looked like a parent propped up a nearly unconscious female.

Jan found a wheelchair and helped the other two plop the girl into it. "What's going on?" Her first thought was a possible drug overdose.

"Regina is my roommate and yesterday she thought she had flu. Today I could hardly wake her."

"Are you her mother?" Jan asked the older woman.

"I'm her dorm mother. I've put a call in to her parents in Missouri and I have authority to have her treated."

"Let's get her inside." A million possibilities raced through Jan's head, but the one thought that kept coming back because of the flu scenario was meningitis. Dorms required first-year students to get vaccinated against it, but it wasn't one hundred percent foolproof. "Regina! Turn your head for me."

The girl moaned with the effort. "My head is killing me."

"Is your neck stiff?"

"Uh-Huh."

Jan wheeled her into room one and, with the help of the other women, undressed her and put a hospital gown on her. As if things weren't bad enough, petechiae around her lower extremities didn't bode well for her diagnosis. She hoped it was a rash, but when she pressed her thumb over the area, the skin didn't blanch like a normal rash would have. Worst-case scenario, this wasn't just potential meningitis, it was possibly the most virulent form of meningitis—bacterial.

The bacteria released endotoxin into the blood stream, making the white blood cells sticky. The "sticky" WBCs damaged the lining of the vessels, causing multiple tiny blood clots to form throughout the body, while disrupting the natural clotting process. The result was leakage of blood into the surrounding tissue, causing the petechiae. If left unchecked, major organ damage would soon follow from the tiny rogue clots.

She stuck her head out the door. "Carmen, ask Dr. Riordan to come quickly."

Before Jan could check the moaning patient's vital signs, Gavin appeared at the bedside. His quick assessment concurred with her worst suspicions.

"Let's do a lumbar puncture. Start an IV. Draw electrolytes, liver and renal panels. Get a blood count and coags." He strode to the exam room door. "Carmen, order a stat chest X-ray and an MRI." He looked back at Jan as she hustled around the bedside, preparing to insert the intravenous line but stopping long enough to take in his concerned expression. "Call me as soon as you're set up for the lumbar puncture."

Ready to place the tourniquet around the young woman's arm, Jan nodded. Her touch set off the previously lethargic patient. Though acting confused, the girl swiped combatively at Jan's hand.

"I'm going to ask you to hold her still for me while I get the IV in place," she said to the other women. One held her arms and the other her legs, and Jan successfully inserted the IV, obtained several vials of blood for the labs and started the intravenous infusion. "Watch her for me while I send these to the lab and get the lumbar-puncture kit, please," she said on her way out the door. "Don't let her dislodge the IV."

They both nodded with anxious expressions. When she reached the nurses' station, Gavin was already instructing Carmen to find a room in the ICU. "As soon as I get the spinal fluid, get her upstairs—she needs constant observation."

Jan knew one-to-one care was next to impossible in the ER with the heavy patient flow, and the sick college girl, Regina, would need all the help she could get in the next several hours.

As she scuttled back toward the room with the pre-packaged lumbar puncture tray, she nodded at Gavin, who was directing Beck toward another patient room. "Take room four. MVA with multiple lacerations." Did Gavin know something was up, too? Had Carmen told him?

Before heading for the room, Beck glanced at Jan long enough to make her hands get jittery and her legs to turn wobbly. A familiar pang of regret made itself known. She redirected her focus on Regina and the procedure.

With the roommate's help, they placed the patient in a C shape on her left side with knees tucked to her chest. The dorm mother stood on the other side of the bed, holding her hands and attempting to make eye contact.

All the necessary equipment was arranged in the sterile kit. Gavin identified the fourth lumbar vertebra and marked the interspace with a skin-marker pen. While he washed his hands, donned sterile gloves and checked the stylet with the LP needle, Jan washed Regina's lower back with anti-septic solution and draped the area with a sterile field.

Gavin quickly injected local anesthetic, and rechecked the lumbar position, then expertly pushed the lumbar puncture needle through the skin. He advanced the needle until a slight "pop" could be heard, then withdrew the stylet to check for CSF flow. When the first drop appeared, he connected the manometer.

Jan held the top of the device to steady it and enable him to make the initial CSF pressure reading. Sure enough, it was above the normal reading by twenty millimeters.

Instead of the normally clear fluid, the CSF looked cloudy, in keeping with an abundance of white blood cells, serum protein and bacteria. Things looked grim for Regina. They collected more spinal fluid in sterile containers and Jan carefully labeled them for the necessary lab studies—a cell count, glucose, and a culture to find out exactly what bug was making her so sick.

"Let's get some broad-spectrum antibiotics started as fast as the inpatient pharmacy can make them up," he said, entering the order into the computer. "Carmen?" he called over his shoulder. "Is that ICU bed ready yet?"

"Fifteen minutes," she called back. "I'm calling Transportation now."

The sooner the patient was in the ICU the better.

Out of habit, Jan instructed the friends to make sure Regina remained flat on her back after the spinal tap to prevent an increased headache—as though her head didn't hurt enough already. At this point Regina hardly seemed able to move by herself. After assessing the patient's responses, according to the Glascow coma scale, Regina was drifting downward rapidly from when she'd first arrived. Though she still opened her eyes to pain, her speech was confused and she'd quit following verbal commands.

Carmen arrived with the first antibiotic, which had been sent via a pneumatic tube system throughout the hospital, and they attached it as a piggyback to the IVAC right before the orderly arrived to transport Regina to the ICU. It couldn't be soon enough in Jan's opinion as she noticed the petechiae around her ankles had spread to larger areas of purple bruising known as purpura. Not a good sign. Patients had been known to lose fingers and toes and worse from the disseminated clotting.

Beck appeared on scene and offered to accompany the patient to the ICU, allowing Jan to process the specimens and clean up the bedside.

She nodded gratefully, avoiding his eyes.

The last thing Jan heard as they left the department was the roommate's comment. "What's Jeremy going to think? They had that big fight two days ago."

"Call him! Tell him what's going on."

"I'm trying. I haven't been able to get a hold of him."

"Are we allowed to use cellphones in the ER?"

Jan glanced at Gavin. "Here, let me show you where the nurses' lounge is. You can call him from there."

Gavin had heard the conversation too. When Jan returned, he'd finished entering his doctor's notes in the portable computer and shook his head. "Just goes to show we never know when our last chance is, do we?"

Jan nodded in accord.

"I almost let Bethany slip away from me, but I came to my senses before it was too late," he added.

Jan recalled Gavin's close brush with anaphylaxis a year earlier and his future wife's near loss of twins. Within two weeks he'd almost lost everything near and dear to him. He could definitely relate to Jeremy's plight.

"Who knows, in another day or two they may have kissed and made up but, as I see it, that guy is going to have major regrets if they can't contact him." Gavin stared deeply into Jan's eyes, and she couldn't help but think he'd suddenly changed the subject from Regina's boyfriend to her. And Beck.

Beck assisted the ICU nurse and the orderly with transferring the patient to the bed. Regina quietly moaned her protest. He handed the orders to the ICU nurse taking over her care, knowing that Jan would have already called in her transfer report.

He'd told Jan he never wanted to see her again, and had done a great job of staying away from the hospital ever since. Lately, he'd been wrapped up in work with all of the crazy protests over the recent bank robbery and the SWAT team's hand in innocent loss of life. He'd also been putting in a lot of time helping out his partner at home during his recuperation from the gunshot wound and colon surgery. Both things gave him a good excuse to avoid seeing Jan.

He thought the police force and city officials were dead wrong and all screwed up on this new call to revamp SWAT, but nothing came close to the messed-up situation with Jan.

Gavin had been the one to call and mention that he needed another twenty hours before he could sign him off for his official medic update. And, to be honest, he'd missed being at the ER. Though it would be best to stay out of Jan's life, reality forced him back into her world.

He'd found her after all of these years, his attraction to her was as strong as ever, they'd just started to find their way back to the comfort and intensity of their old relationship, then she'd dropped the bombshell about their daughter. Did everything in life have to be so complicated?

Over the years he'd avoided any other real relationships by keeping busy. His years in the military, continuing with the National Guard reserve and finally choosing the most demanding unit in LAPD to build his career, SWAT, had left little room or time for a significant relationship. The cynical joke circulating the unit was, "You're not a real SWAT man until you've had your first divorce."

Divorce wasn't an option for him. If or when he ever got married, it would be for the rest of his life. Something inside had him holding out for that one special person.

Whenever a woman started to protest about his inaccessibility, and they always did around the two-to-three-month mark, he'd use it as an excuse to break things off. So far his system had worked out fine. But he was thirty-one now and still alone. And "alone" didn't seem to fit as well since being around Jan.

Even if things weren't so messed up, the odds would be stacked against them. She'd probably be like every other woman in his life and grow tired of his work schedule and monthly reservists' weekends. Not to mention getting called up for active duty every couple of years. What was the point of thinking about it? Yet he had been, knowing his reserve contract would be up next year. He didn't have to sign on again.

After working the ER for the last four weeks he'd started thinking about using his GI bill to help pay for official physician assistant training. Why not tap into the government money promised for education to all US soldiers in thanks for their service? He deserved it. He'd been so set on becoming a police officer after being discharged from the army that he'd unwisely let the opportunity to get a PA license slip between his fingers. Little did he know what the future would bring.

He'd forgotten how good it felt to do patient care and to make a difference in people's lives. Sure, LAPD's promise to protect and serve was a noble cause, but now medicine seemed more basic and personally gratifying, and it would take him out of the frontline of fire, which would make Jan happy. And why was he even following this line of thought?

Because deep down, when he blocked out all the other noise in his head and was completely honest with himself, he realized that long ago January had made a decision to protect him at all costs. And when he dug deeper into the honesty…well, he knew it had been the best decision for their baby, too. She'd sacrificed everything for him…because she'd loved him.

What's a man supposed to do with the truth?

None of it mattered any more. He'd be shipping out for Afghanistan in two weeks. He'd be gone for six months. There was just no point.

When Beck arrived back in the emergency department he saw Jan in one of the exam rooms, holding a large basin while a patient vomited. With an empathetic expression on her face, she stood nearby, rubbing the patient's back and mumbling no doubt encouraging and comforting words. Why couldn't she be despicable?

The truth was, she was the one woman he'd never forget. And the one woman he'd never have again.

Gavin called him aside and told Beck he'd be assisting the rest of the night with the on-call orthopedic doc he'd just called in. There seemed to be an abundance of broken limbs in the ER tonight.

Relieved he wouldn't be working beside January, he stepped into the first patient's room in time to hear the man let out an excruciating yell as the Ortho doc realigned his dislocated finger.

The situation seemed somehow apropos to Beck's mood.

Two hours later, word was Regina had lapsed into a coma in the ICU. Carmen repeated the news at the doctors' and nurses' station and Gavin heard it along with everyone else.

Apparently stuck on the more esoteric aspect of the tragedy regarding Regina and her boyfriend, he turned to Jan and said, "I wonder if they got a hold of her guy? That just goes to show that sometimes, if you hesitate in love, you lose," he mumbled, shaking his head and heading toward his office.

He must have been talking to Carmen.

Before entering the room, he turned and raised his index finger. "Remember where you heard that."

Only one person's face came to mind when Gavin dispensed his pearls of wisdom.

She scanned the ED and found Beck examining a possible broken arm in room seven. Gavin's point had been well taken. Even if all was lost with Beck, she'd never forgive herself if she didn't at least try to make him understand before he left again. If she didn't ask—no, beg—for his forgiveness. She'd never find the self-respect she'd been searching for all these years.

Jan had also promised to never lie to Beck again. Her time was running short. Soon he'd be gone. After searching her heart for the last week, she knew that she had to tell him.

Jan had found out from Carmen that Saturday was Beck's day off from both the ER and LAPD, and since she had a day off from the hospital, there was no excuse not to take advantage. Thirteen years ago she'd squandered her chance to be honest and tell him exactly how she'd felt. He was leaving, and she didn't have time to waste. After so long the thought that today was the day to bare her soul made her heart shimmy.

She dressed carefully in her favorite colorful dress with a halter top. Since it was her last stand with Beck, she wanted it to be memorable. She went all out and put on make-up, lining her lips a shade darker than the rose lipstick she wore and making sure the mascara was water-proof. The thought of getting emotional and having black streaks run down her cheeks wasn't the least bit appealing.

Today she'd also wear her contact lenses. If Beck were to stand his ground about never wanting to see her again, she wanted him to remember her without her glasses, vain as that may be.

She glided her hand over the tumbling butterflies in her belly and smoothed the skirt across her hips. She turned to make sure her exposed back didn't have any surprise bug bites on it, and while she was in the neighborhood she checked out her own backside. Not bad. Not bad at all.

At three in the afternoon, with one last deep breath she slipped on her heeled sandals, grabbed her purse then headed for the door. She'd purposely waited until the afternoon since he'd worked the night before. She wanted to make sure he'd had enough sleep to lessen the odds he'd be cranky with her.

Starting up her car, she searched her memories but couldn't recall one time that Beck had ever been cranky with her, not even when she'd refused to tell him what he'd needed to hear the night before he'd left for bootcamp. Back in high school, and even recently, until she'd dropped the bombshell on him about Meghan, he'd always seemed glad to see her and had treated her with respect. Until she'd proved she didn't deserve it. Well, things were about to change. It was time to reclaim her self-respect, and hopefully his as well.

Life shouldn't depend on whether or not Beck forgave her, but it sure would make it easier for her to forgive herself if he did.

As she drove, she wondered how he'd respond to seeing her at his door a second time, especially after she got through telling him why she was there.

Beck had forgotten what a good night's sleep felt like. He'd tossed and turned and given up some time around seven. After a rigorous workout, he'd mowed the lawn and showered. What he needed was some mindless distraction. Since sex was out of the question, he was grateful a baseball game was on TV.

Halfway through his lunch of a ham sandwich and a cold beer, someone knocked on his door. He debated throwing on a shirt, but decided it was too much effort. Maybe he wouldn't even answer the door. The doorbell rang. Waiting to make sure the batter hadn't hit a home run, he sidled toward the door with eyes trained on the television. Still unsure whether or not to waste his time opening the door, he looked through the peephole.

A mini-jolt of adrenaline detonated in his chest as he assessed the colorfully dressed woman on the other side. He'd flat out told her he never wanted to see her again, and here she was on his doorstep, looking as sexy as a film star.

He should be angry.

Feeling more pleasantly surprised than irritated, he swung the door open a tad quicker than he'd meant, then made up for it by using a casual drawl. "What brings you here?"

"I know I'm the last person you want to see, but may I come in?" With over-bright eyes, she seemed determined. Not a good sign. If her manner was any indication, she'd come to his house on a mission, not to pay a social visit.

So why wasn't she wearing a bra?

"Sure." He stepped aside. "Want a beer or a sandwich?"

"Oh, no thanks." Latching a lock of hair behind an ear, suddenly she seemed less sure of herself as she edged toward his sofa.

Though he'd tidied up the yard, he'd neglected the house. All the military gear he'd pulled from storage sat piled and ready to pack in one corner of the room. When he hadn't been able to sleep last night, he'd gotten out his easel and worked on the abstract portrait he couldn't get out of his head. What would Jan say if she saw it? He turned the canvas to face the wall, hoping she hadn't noticed it was of her, then bunched up the newspapers covering the couch. He used the remote to shut off the TV, and gestured for her to sit. She did, but primly and on the edge with hands folded in her lap, acting the complete opposite of how she looked. What was up with that?

"Look, you've got to have something. I'm eating. How about a glass of water at least?"

Her tense expression cracked a bit as she tried out a half-hearted smile. "OK. Water's fine."

He couldn't help but notice how sexy she looked in her knee-length sundress. Her bare shoulders practically called out to be caressed and kissed, and the natural slope of her breasts beneath the smooth fabric made him suddenly need a glass of water, too. Like the old days, she'd dressed like a birthday present, all bright colors, ribbons and bows and sparkles, and he suddenly wanted to unwrap her.

Taking a minute to gather his composure in the kitchen, Beck filled two cups with cold filtered water from the refrigerator and forced a more businesslike frame of mind. She'd obviously come there for a reason, though his first thoughts were more in keeping with seduction. Not very likely. He made a wise decision—he'd keep his mouth shut and see what was on her mind.

After handing over the glass, he sat a careful distance from her on the couch. The half-eaten ham sandwich had somehow lost its appeal. He gulped down half the water.

"What's up?" he said, feigning aloofness.

Jan scratched her upper lip and took a breath. "The thing is, I originally came over here to ask you to forgive me."

Fighting off a sudden wave of empathy, he bit out the first words in his head. "Forgive you for not telling me you were pregnant, or for giving our baby away, or for possibly never telling me a thing if we hadn't happened to meet again? Which exactly is it you want me to forgive?"

He wasn't prepared for the toll his outburst would take. She'd gone directly to "falling apart" mode. Aw, hell.

Tears brimmed in her eyes, making the blue more intense and all the more beautiful. "Please, forgive me." She reached for his forearm and squeezed. He tensed with the unwanted electricity of her touch.

"You don't need my forgiveness, January."

"Yes, I do."

Caught in the exhausting battle going on in his head about whether to tell her he'd already taken the first steps to forgiving her or to continue holding a dwindling grudge, the silence yawned on. He stared at the floor.

"I figured something out on the drive over here," she said in a wavering voice. "I couldn't expect you to forgive me when I had never forgiven myself. And you know what? I might never have been able to if I hadn't seen a well-adjusted and wonderfully bright girl the other day."

January searched his face until she captured his gaze and held it. She'd made a good point. Meghan was well adjusted and obviously happy with her life. Hell, hadn't he been thinking that very thing every single night when he'd searched for peace of mind in his sleeplessness? He'd already decided to drop his efforts to pursue visiting rights and disrupt Meghan's life. He clamped his jaw, not ready to let her off the hook so easily.

"Yes, she was our birth daughter, but she has two of the most loving adoptive parents anyone could ever hope for. Surely you can appreciate that, Beck. No one has ever laid a hand on her, like your father used to do with you. No one has ever tried to orchestrate every stage of her life, like my mother did with me. She's been given the freedom we both deserved but never had as kids."

"But without us," he reminded her.

Jan swallowed and, with trembling fingers, wiped away a tear running down her cheek. He sat numbly watching. What kind of monster had he turned into?

"Look, I hear what you're saying," Beck continued, "but I've got a whole lot of feelings to work through first."

Amazingly, she'd kept herself from completely crumbling. She took a sip of water and turned back to him. "I can't speak for you, but I know I would have been a lousy parent at seventeen. Meghan wouldn't have gotten the love and attention she deserved once I realized she wasn't a doll to play dress-up with. I didn't have a clue about life, Beck, let alone being a mother. You've got to understand that though I took the wrong approach, I did it for the right reason." She stared at him for a second. He still couldn't bring himself to let her off the hook. "And today, on the drive over, I finally realized that. I wish you would, too."

Fighting off an uncomfortable wave of remorse, he found his voice, though his thoughts weren't clear or in any particular order. "What am I supposed to do, January?"

"I've asked your forgiveness, and until you can find it in your heart to forgive me, you'll be stuck in time. It's finally dawned on me—forgiving myself doesn't depend on you. It's been long overdue, and you know what? I'm letting myself off the hook. No more guilt. That kid of ours is thriving…without us. Guess what, Beck? I did the right thing." She stared at him. He sat stoically. "Look, I'll do what you want. I'll never see you again. I promise. Even if you do forgive me, I'll stay out of your life, if that's what you want. But for your own good, you won't be whole until you forgive me and move on."

"I'm not sure that's what I need. I get that you made a tough decision on your own. But, you see, that's the part where I get hung up. I wanted to be in on the decision in the first place." He needed another drink of water though the unsteady hand that held the glass accented his bitterness. "You cut me out of your life. Out of my daughter's life. What am I supposed to do about that?"

She briefly closed her eyes then ruefully glanced at him. "Let it go. Forgive me. What's done is done."

Sadness loomed like a cloud, heavy on his mind. His mother's favorite saying echoed in his head—"Grant me the serenity to accept that which I cannot change." He struggled to say the words over a thickened throat. "I'm trying, January," he said hoarsely. "I'm not sure I'm ready to do that."

They sat quietly stewing in their individual thoughts for several seconds. With his eyes burning and his chest as heavy and tight as when he wore his bulletproof vest, he was amazed when he noticed her subtle floral scent. And as confused as he felt about their past and their questionable future, he wanted to bury his face in her neck and inhale until his lungs burst. Why did she have that power to torture and titillate him simultaneously?

Because she was the one woman—

"There's one more thing," she said, pulling him out of his thoughts as she started to stand. "Regardless of whether or not you can find it in your heart to forgive me, since you're going away and I promised myself I'd never lie to you again…" She faced him and, with tender, sky-blue eyes, gazed steadily into his face. Then, with a flurry of breathy words she said, "I want you to know that I still love you."

CHAPTER TEN

GOOSE-BUMPS cascaded from the top of Jan's head over her shoulders, down her arms to her fingertips. There, she'd said it. She'd just admitted the deepest secret she'd been hoarding for over a decade. It was the reason she hadn't been able to love her ex-husband. The reason she hadn't been able to move on with her life. She loved Beck Braxton and she always would.

Now she'd have to face his reaction, whatever it was, and live with it.

Holding her breath, she dared to look into his eyes and saw a slightly surprised, yet receptive glint. The air whooshed back into her lungs. Early signs of a smile twitched at the edges of his mouth. Would he laugh at her outrageous confession?

Long fingers wrapped around her wrist and pulled her near. Jan braced herself, splaying her hands across Beck's chest. He hadn't worn a shirt and she'd tried with all her power to ignore that fact when she'd arrived. Now she was touching him and the energy transferring itself from his body through her fingertips was riveting. She loved the solid feel of his muscles and the smooth skin covering them.

She'd bared her soul and, instead of being rejected, he wanted to hold her. Maybe she'd survive this day after all.

She searched for the soft side of his neck, the spot she'd been denied the last time he'd held her, and kissed him there. Heat and intensity radiated from his chest through the thin fabric of her halter neck. Her breasts tightened in response, and she pulled herself closer, wrapping her arms around his neck. Air, as if forgiveness, released from his lungs in a long slow exhalation.

She shivered with anticipation. "Does this mean you forgive me?" Looking up, she saw him holding back a raw reaction to her declaration of love and plea for exoneration by biting his lip. If only she could know what was going through his mind. Would everything work out after all? If she went by touch alone she'd say yes, but his glassy hazel eyes gazed downward and it made her wonder if what he was preparing to say would hurt.

"Damn, lady. You confuse the hell out of me."

"I don't mean to. I just couldn't let you go away again without you knowing how I felt."

"You love me?"

She nodded and wriggled closer to him. "I do. I never stopped."

He lifted his brows. "Then I guess I have to forgive you. The truth is, no one in the world has sacrificed more for me than you, January. As much as you hurt me, you had to hurt ten times worse."

His face went blurry. Relief rolled through every muscle in her body. Finally he understood.

Beck's mouth clamped down on hers and she felt each ounce of remaining doubt dissipate. They melded in a long, ravenous kiss. Magically her halter top came tumbling down and in what seemed like a heartbeat they found themselves naked and entwined on his bed.

Heat and sensation, soft with hard, tender and rough, every caress built on the next as they expressed their feelings through touch. Cosmetic scents mingled with nature's earthiness. The sweet taste of kisses blended with the salty tang of flesh.

Nothing could sate the flourishing desire between them. Their hands couldn't keep them close enough. Their kisses weren't deep enough. Only their joining as man and woman would satisfy the abyss of need.

Jan straddled Beck's hips and dipped down so he could kiss and suckle her breasts. She arched and stretched with the delicious sensations coiling throughout her body. Hot hands directed her hips down to where he waited, hard and erect. His intimate touches tested whether she was ready for him. Excitement soared when he pressed at her entrance. He opened her and placed himself inside as she gently rocked over him. Exquisite warmth and firm pressure filled her. She bent to capture his mouth with a soulful kiss as they moved, slowly at first, together.

Greedy urges to devour him competed with subtle sensations begging to draw out the delicacy.

Take it easy. Savor the sensations.

Bursts of untamed throbbing soon overshadowed the long luxurious strokes. With sensations burning across her skin, Jan bucked and met Beck's thrusts, over and over.

He rolled her onto her back and she wrapped her legs around his hips so he could drive deeper. Fisting the sheets, she lost all inhibition, begging him to go faster, harder, deeper still.

Beck lowered himself over her and held her face to delve into her eyes as they made love belly to belly, pelvis to pelvis. His piercing hooded stare reached to her very center, squeezing her heart until she thought she'd die.

"I love you," he said huskily.

With each thrust he claimed her as his, leaving her useless for any other man in the universe. "Beck," she whimpered.

He went completely still. With an unwavering gaze and clenched jaw he promised, "I'm yours."

"For ever," she added.

He smiled. "Since the first day I met you."

He tilted her hips and thrust again. Heat fanned and flamed, bursting through every pore of her skin. Beck surged deeper and deeper until he blinked and moaned. He shuddered and came just before her, but continued thrusting until everything locked tight and molten spasms rolled through her center.

Jan licked her lips and savored every last shiver and roll, loving Beck's weight pressed against her body. The man she loved. The man who'd finally forgiven her.

After a bit, he nibbled her earlobe and rolled aside then gathered her close. She cuddled next to him, equally loving this moment. His life force beat steadily beneath her ear, mesmerizing and lulling her until she fell asleep.

Jan wasn't sure how long she'd slept, but when she woke up Beck was out of bed, dressed and pacing. She sat up. The room edged toward twilight.

"What time is it?" she asked.

"Six," he said, coming to a stop. "I need to take you home."

Had he changed his mind? Dread crept like an injured animal across her mind. Don't panic. "Did you get called into work or something?"

"No. I've been making plans."

"Plans?"

"Yeah. Plans about not re-enlisting after this tour. Plans about transferring out of SWAT. Plans about using the GI education bill to get my PA license so I can work in an ER and really make a difference."

"Sex really energizes you, I guess," she said, trying to keep things light and work through the implications of his brainstorm.

He chuckled. "I've got more plans, too."

"Really? 'Cause that sounds like a lot of plans for one afternoon."

"Pack your bags. We're going to Las Vegas. I'm not leaving the country without you being my wife."

"Fantastical!" Though stunned to the point of breathlessness, and riding a thrill so high she could almost touch heaven, practicality set in. "But haven't you forgotten something?"

"If I can get time off work, I'm sure you can, too."

Still reeling with excitement, she screwed up her face and gave him an impudent glare.

"Look, I promise when I come back from Afghanistan we'll have a real wedding. A big wedding, if that's what you want. But we don't have time for that now."

She put her hands on her hips and continued with her call-my-bluff glare.

A brief confused expression moved like a passing cloud over his face. Understanding dawned and the look quickly changed to a warm smile. The most gorgeous smile Jan had ever seen, where the brackets around his mouth turned into deep dimples and his eyes twinkled though they were scrunched tight.

Switching gears from "Hurry up" to "This is the most important moment in our lives" he sat on the edge of the bed, took her hand, drew it to his warm, full lips and kissed her knuckles.

"January," he whispered, gazing lovingly into her eyes. "Will you marry me?"

Two months later Jan parked in the employees' parking lot and smiled when her gaze happened on the ortho tech and his main squeeze, necking by their car. It made her long to be in Beck's arms again. She remembered their last kiss, when she'd had to send him off for duty with the National Guard. She'd bitten back her fear and kissed him with her soul, not caring that it was broad daylight and there had been hundreds of people milling around, saying their good-byes to loved ones. They were man and wife and would spend the rest of their lives together, if he made it safe and sound through his tour of duty.

Somehow she'd survive the unbearable months since then and they'd pick up where they'd left off. Deeply in love. Devoted to one another. Crazy in lust! She sighed and practically floated past the Mercy Hospital parking-lot lovers, examining her wedding band. Though simple, it was solid and real, like their love, and she knew that wher-ever he was he wore the matching ring. That thought had helped her through the tough times. Refusing to accept any other ending, one day they'd never be apart again.

In the meantime, she'd have to settle for e-mail and phone

calls, and when she was really lucky an occasional web-cam visit. And in between she'd been communing with her maker. Especially since her body had started whispering to her about wonderful things to come. Mostly she'd ignored the hints, nowhere near ready to deal with the possibilities.

No sooner had Jan arrived in the bustling ED than Carmen started counting off orders. "We need a blood gas in room three and a central venous line dressing change in room seven. Room two is passing a kidney stone and is waiting for an IVP before Gavin decides if he needs to go to the OR to have a stent placed. He could use another pain shot. If you've got a chance, room five needs some stitches removed."

Jan glanced around the department, and not a single soul was sitting down. Constant movement in and out of the exam rooms by doctors, nurses, and techs foretold how her evening would go. And she was glad! The busier she was, the quicker time would pass. Days would turn into weeks and weeks into months and in four months, she'd be holding Beck in her arms again.

She stopped momentarily and inhaled the familiar odor of harsh hospital disinfectant mixed with the odor of an endless sea of bodies spilling through the ER doors. Something she'd smelled regularly made her queasy today.

After tending to the kidney-stone patient's pain med needs, Jan gathered a blood-gas kit and headed for room three.

She'd use the radial artery for her sample, so a smaller and shorter needle would be fine. The test would assess the respiratory function and acid-base status of this first-visit patient suspected of having emphysema.

Jan found a frail, bone-thin woman who looked well beyond her stated sixty-five years. Her history revealed a two-pack-a-day cigarette habit of approximately forty years. Though she'd noticed shortness of breath for the last couple of years, today, according to her daughter, the patient had started laughing while watching television. The laugh had turned into her usual rattling cough then progressed until the patient hadn't been able to breathe. It had scared her enough to bring her to the ER. Jan's job, by collecting the specimen, was to find out how compromised her lungs were.

After explaining the procedure and using aseptic technique, Jan opened the blood-gas kit. She filled the provided plastic bag with ice, then rolled a towel and extended the patient's wrist across it. After locating the arterial pulse, she cleansed the area thoroughly with antiseptic then donned gloves and fixed the artery in place between her index and middle fingers. She warned the patient it would be uncomfortable and, using a heparinized syringe, she introduced the needle through the skin and deeper into the pulsing vein.

"Ouch," the patient said, dutifully holding her wrist still.

"I'm sorry," Jan whispered in deep concentration. When the syringe spontaneously filled with bright red blood, she knew she'd hit her mark. After attaining 2 ml, she withdrew the needle and immediately placed a pressure dressing on the patient's wrist. "Press on that for five minutes." The patient used her free hand to do as she'd been instructed.

Jan carefully removed any air bubbles from the syringe then utilized the safe needle disposing system before labeling and placing the specimen on ice for transport to the lab.

After making sure the patient applied enough pressure to her arterial wound, Jan left the room just as the orderly came to transport the patient to Radiology for a chest X-ray.

"Don't let up on that pressure for five minutes," Jan re-iterated as the sparrow-thin woman was helped into a wheelchair.

"I won't," the patient said in a wheezy voice followed by a phlegmy cough.

Already planning her central line dressing change on the next patient, if she was lucky the evening would be non-stop and soon she'd get to go home and cross off one more day on her countdown-to-Beck calendar. One more day closer to seeing her husband.

She still thrilled at the thought that she and Beck were married. They'd opted for an intimate gimmick-free chapel in Las Vegas, where a pastor had been available to perform the wedding ceremony instead of a justice of the peace. And though their witnesses had been total strangers, she and Beck repeated their vows as if no one else existed in the world.

He'd promised a big wedding when he returned, but she'd rather spend the money on a special honeymoon. Though she was pretty sure Carmen would never speak to her again if she didn't at least throw a party!

By eight o'clock Jan was ready for her dinner break. The day had been warm and she suspected the night would be balmy. Rather than spend her precious break time cooped up in the nurses' lounge, she decided to take her brown-bag dinner outside.

Usually, she'd fill a foam cup with the false energy of hot coffee and cream, but tonight she opted for cranberry juice and headed for the ER exit. Finding her favorite hideout bench surrounded by bushes, she sat down and opened her sandwich pack. While she ate, she went over her last phone call from Beck in her mind. He was safe, in a relatively inactive insurgent area. He'd been very excited about receiving a letter from Meghan and had read Jan every word. Before hanging up, he'd told her again how much he loved and missed her, then whispered a few things he intended to do to her once he came home. As always, she'd jokingly told him she'd never forgive him if he didn't keep himself safe. Then had come the long torturous silence before they'd had to say goodbye and hang up. She'd make it through this one last separation. Then they'd never be apart again.

A few bites into her meal she saw a young woman hustle by, carrying a cardboard box.

Curiosity got the better of her and Jan peered out from her secluded spot to see a girl, seemingly torn about leaving the box by the emergency department doors.

A chill drove down Jan's spine. She rushed toward her and heard what sounded like a mewing kitten.

"Let me help you," Jan said.

The young woman stood right in front of the ER notice with the official logo for the Safe Surrender project. Mercy Hospital, and every other ER in Los Angeles since 2001, had been deemed a baby drop-off point to assuage the horrendous act of leaving unwanted babies at random spots around the city or, worse, in Dumpsters.

The girl looked as though she wanted to bolt.

Jan carefully opened the flaps of the box and wanted to cry when she saw what was inside. A precious newborn. Had she been born today?

The law clearly stated that the mother could drop off her baby within 72 hours of birth with no questions asked, as long as she handed it to someone and the infant was unharmed.

"Come inside. Let us see to your needs," Jan said.

The girl shook her head vehemently.

"We can help you. Don't you want to make sure you don't hemorrhage or have any complications?"

It was optional for the mother to fill out a health history, but more importantly the mother could be issued a bracelet and a matching one was placed on her baby to allow for a cooling-off period during which she could change her mind and get her baby back. After thirty days without contact, the baby would be put up for adoption.

The young brunette loped into the night. "I'm OK," she called over her shoulder. "Just take care of the baby."

"What's your name?"

"Andrea."

Jan gulped in air. Adrenaline shot out of every organ in her body. Chasing after a runaway teenage mother was not an option. The baby must come first.

From the look of the little one it was no more than a few hours old. What was she supposed to do?

A million questions rushed through Jan's head, but the biggest question occupying her brain was what had driven the girl to leave her baby and run?

The plethora of questions would have to wait, and would most likely go unanswered. A newborn needed medical attention, and Jan would see to it the infant got the best Mercy Hospital could give.

Jan swooped down and gingerly lifted the baby from the box lined with newspapers. The baby still had vernix on her skin and, peeking under the gaping disposable diaper, Jan saw that the umbilical cord was long and still attached. It could have been chewed off by the looks of the jagged cut.

Had the girl gone through labor and delivered by herself?

Sorrow flooded Jan's heart. The poor babies. Both of them. She looked ruefully at the infant, her chest constricting. "Poor darlin', let me get you inside."

Before she stepped into the ER Jan glanced around the parking lot for any sign of the teenager. Then she rummaged through the box, hoping to find a note. Nothing.

The baby would start out her life motherless and abandoned. How could the mother do that? Whoa. Hold on there. Couldn't the same be said about her? Until she'd convinced him otherwise, Beck had felt the same way about what Jan had done. How could Jan possibly judge this girl? Maybe the drop-off mother had done the wrong thing, but she'd done it for the right reason…to give her baby a chance.

Before her heart could break she muttered, "Come on, sweetie. Let's get you cleaned up."

Jan caused quite a stir rushing into the ER holding an abandoned baby. "What do we do now?" she asked.

"I'll give Children's Services a call." Carmen went right into policy and procedure mode, taking just enough time to glance at the baby, a girl. Carmen mouthed "Cute" while waiting for the phone to be answered.

"We've got to keep her warm. Becky," Jan called to another nurse. "Can you get a blanket from the warmer, please?"

Jan held the baby snugly to her chest to help keep her body temperature up and to let the baby hear a heartbeat. The infant deserved nothing less.

A sudden memory of the first time she'd held Meghan flashed into her mind. The incredible wonder of holding a life that had grown inside her body had been overwhelming. Bitter-sweet emotions had made her weep, knowing she'd have to say goodbye to her baby almost as quickly as she'd said hello. The nurse had been warm-hearted and compassionate and had allowed her to hold Meghan as long as she'd wanted. Eventually, reality had kicked in. Jan had promised her baby to an eagerly awaiting couple, who didn't deserve to be kept waiting another moment. They would be the ones to bond with her daughter. They'd earned the right.

Uncomfortable prickles behind her eyes preceded blurred vision. The infant squirmed. Jan held her close and kissed the top of her head. Could she dare go through a pregnancy again? Lately, her tender breasts and bloated abdomen had had her thinking she might not have the choice, but she hadn't tested herself…yet.

"Do we have any formula? How about dextrose water, at least?"

"I'm calling the pediatric doctor on call," another nurse said, picking up the phone and dialing.

"Becky, can you bring a large basin and fill it with warm water? I need to clean this little one up."

Becky nodded, hustling across the ER.

Once the pediatric doctor on call had been notified, Jan went to work, cleaning up the baby. Long, silky brown-tinged hair lay stuck to her slightly pointed head. Her dark blue eyes were trying to open, but kept shutting just as quickly as they popped open. The round face and flat nose weren't her most beautiful features but newborns were never very pretty. And most importantly she had ten perfect fingers and ten perfect toes. And Jan kissed each one.

From what Jan could gather, this baby was flawless,

though a bit scrawny. A hearty wail belied her prematurity. The infant had definitely been born early, but Jan would leave just how early up to the peds doc to figure out.

"Don't you worry about a thing, munchkin. Now that you're all cleaned up, I'll feed you." The baby stretched and jerked and made another mewing sound. It was definitely time to feed.

Holding her close, Jan eased the bottle nipple into her mouth and was relieved to see a strong sucking reflex, which turned into a gobble fest. There was no telling how long the baby had been in the world, but she was definitely hungry.

For the first time in thirteen years, Jan let herself wonder what it would be like to have a baby of her own. A baby she'd never let go of. Maybe it was time to take that pregnancy test.

The newborn stopped sucking briefly, her little tongue pressed at the perfectly round opening of her Cupid's-bow lips. Earnest eyes ventured open in the dimmed exam room. Jan smiled. "Hi, precious. Want to be friends?" Jan pulled two bracelets from her pocket. One was meant for the dropped-off infant and the other for the mother. Jan decided to keep Andrea's bracelet for her, in case she changed her mind.

The baby girl seemed to be staring intently at Jan, though she knew newborns couldn't focus. "Your eyes look so clear. If I got to name you, I'd call you Claire." Maybe if she had another daughter one day, she'd name her that.

The peds doctor showed up just before Jan finished feeding the baby. The white-haired doctor reached out large hands and smiled. "Let's have a look."

When Children's Services arrived, Jan spent half an

hour answering their questions. Afterwards, they followed the baby and the pediatric nurse upstairs to the neonatal unit to complete their paperwork. Sensing a tremendous and immediate loss, Jan made her decision to buy a pregnancy test on her way home from work. And since she wanted to share the event with her husband, she'd e-mail Beck to call her as soon as she got home.

At three in the morning, Jan's phone rang. It was Beck, and it was two p.m. Afghan time.

"I got your e-mail. Is everything all right?" he asked.

"Yes. Everything is wonderful."

"I love you."

"I love you, too."

"I'll be home in four more months. I can't wait to get you naked." His voice contained a smile.

She grinned back. "You'll have to beat me to it!"

They laughed, then grew quiet.

"What's up?"

Jan repeated the entire story of her baby adventure.

"Incredible," he said.

"Yeah. And there's something else pretty incredible to tell you, too."

"What's that?"

"I've just taken a home pregnancy test and we're going to be parents…again."

"Are you kidding me?" Then she heard him hoot and yell to another soldier, "I'm going to be a dad!"

Finally feeling ready to venture into the unknown realm of parenting, as long as it was with Beck, she grinned so widely her eyes watered. "So what do you think?"

"Woo-hoo. It's fantastical!"

EPILOGUE

"FALL in!" the lieutenant ordered.

No sooner had the Delta division of the National Guard disembarked from their military plane in Los Alamitos amidst cheers and screams than they were asked to line up on the airport asphalt.

The lieutenant stepped up to the microphone and went into a speech about their service.

Jan stretched her neck for a glimpse of Beck, her heart pounding in her chest. There he was! She'd recognize his physique anywhere. Could he see her? She primped her now longer hair with newly added highlights, and smoothed the carnation-pink blouse she'd worn for the occasion.

All the gathering families grew quiet as the officer paused.

"I'm going to make this short and sweet. This is your last order on a job well done. At ease, men!"

Chaos broke loose as families pushed through the barriers. Wives and lovers, mothers and fathers, children and grandchildren frantically tried to find their soldiers. Jan kept her eyes on the prize and snaked through the crowd toward Beck, getting jostled and bumped along the way.

He hadn't seen her yet. He scanned the crowd, hand over

eyes, to lessen the glare. It made her grin to the point of cheek cramps.

I'm not going to cry, she chanted over and over in her head. "Beck!" she called.

He heard his name, but hadn't seen her yet.

She waved. "Beck! Over here!" She waved again.

His face brightened and a huge smile beamed from his face. He was the most beautiful sight she could ever imagine. She rushed to him, almost bumping into a young child who stood by her parents while they hugged. She scooted around her and lunged forward.

Beck met her halfway. They rushed together in a tight embrace. "I can't believe it," he said, lifting her off the ground and spinning her around.

She'd promised not to cry but the dam broke. Tears streamed down her cheeks, though she smiled and kissed him. "Me neither," she said. "It feels like forever since you left."

"You look so fantastic," he said, placing her back on the ground.

"So do you." She squeezed his arms and patted his stomach. "Maybe a little skinny, but we'll work on that," she said with a nervous laugh.

He grinned. "I love you," he said, and kissed her again.

"I love you, too." She kissed him back.

Only then did Jan realize a local television news crew was recording their entire encounter. It didn't matter. Nothing mattered except Beck.

"How much did you miss him?" one of the reporters asked.

"This much," she said. With careless abandon she grabbed Beck's face and kissed him deeply. A rousing hoot rose from the film crew.

"Today is welcome-home day at Los Alamitos for the Delta unit of the National Guard after a six-month stint in the middle east. As you can see, this wife is happy to have her soldier home."

Realizing her red-hot kiss would be on the evening TV news, Jan didn't care. In front of God and her country she planted another mind-melting kiss on her man.

After Jan and Beck ended the kiss and the initial uproar settled down, the news reporters found someone else to interview. She and Beck hugged and pressed against each other, making sure they were real, that this moment wasn't a dream. His hand came to rest on her new baby bump.

"How's our kid?"

"Doing great."

As if he knew she needed reassurance, he held her hand and gazed into her eyes. "You're going to be a great mother."

"Thank you. And you're going to be a great dad. Now, let's go home," she said.

Arms around each other, they walked toward the parking lot. Jan smiled, filled to bursting with love for her man. Overwhelmed with all the wonderful feelings swirling in her head, she found it hard to find her voice.

"I wanted to get your opinion," she said. "I was thinking it would be really great to have our official wedding party after our baby is born."

Squeezing her shoulder, he gave a knowing look, one that showed he understood. She'd waited to make the decision with him this time, as she would with every decision from here on out.

Beck smiled and replied, "That sounds like a perfect plan."

0309 Gen Std HB

MILLS & BOON®
Pure reading pleasure™

APRIL 2009 HARDBACK TITLES

ROMANCE

The Billionaire's Bride of Convenience	Miranda Lee
Valentino's Love-Child	Lucy Monroe
Ruthless Awakening	Sara Craven
The Italian Count's Defiant Bride	Catherine George
The Multi-Millionaire's Virgin Mistress	Cathy Williams
The Innocent's Dark Seduction	Jennie Lucas
Bedded for Pleasure, Purchased for Pregnancy	Carol Marinelli
The Diakos Baby Scandal	Natalie Rivers
Salzano's Captive Bride	Daphne Clair
The Tuscan Tycoon's Pregnant Housekeeper	Christina Hollis
Outback Heiress, Surprise Proposal	Margaret Way
Honeymoon with the Boss	Jessica Hart
His Princess in the Making	Melissa James
Dream Date with the Millionaire	Melissa McClone
Maid in Montana	Susan Meier
Hired: The Italian's Bride	Donna Alward
The Greek Billionaire's Love-Child	Sarah Morgan
Greek Doctor, Cinderella Bride	Amy Andrews

HISTORICAL

His Reluctant Mistress	Joanna Maitland
The Earl's Forbidden Ward	Bronwyn Scott
The Rake's Inherited Courtesan	Ann Lethbridge

MEDICAL™

The Rebel Surgeon's Proposal	Margaret McDonagh
Temporary Doctor, Surprise Father	Lynne Marshall
Dr Velascos' Unexpected Baby	Dianne Drake
Falling for her Mediterranean Boss	Anne Fraser

MILLS & BOON®
Pure reading pleasure™

APRIL 2009 LARGE PRINT TITLES

ROMANCE

The Greek Tycoon's Disobedient Bride	Lynne Graham
The Venetian's Midnight Mistress	Carole Mortimer
Ruthless Tycoon, Innocent Wife	Helen Brooks
The Sheikh's Wayward Wife	Sandra Marton
The Italian's Christmas Miracle	Lucy Gordon
Cinderella and the Cowboy	Judy Christenberry
His Mistletoe Bride	Cara Colter
Pregnant: Father Wanted	Claire Baxter

HISTORICAL

Miss Winbolt and the Fortune Hunter	Sylvia Andrew
Captain Fawley's Innocent Bride	Annie Burrows
The Rake's Rebellious Lady	Anne Herries

MEDICAL™

A Baby for Eve	Maggie Kingsley
Marrying the Millionaire Doctor	Alison Roberts
His Very Special Bride	Joanna Neil
City Surgeon, Outback Bride	Lucy Clark
A Boss Beyond Compare	Dianne Drake
The Emergency Doctor's Chosen Wife	Molly Evans

0409 Gen Std HB

MAY 2009 HARDBACK TITLES

ROMANCE

The Greek Tycoon's Blackmailed Mistress	Lynne Graham
Ruthless Billionaire, Forbidden Baby	Emma Darcy
Constantine's Defiant Mistress	Sharon Kendrick
The Sheikh's Love-Child	Kate Hewitt
The Boss's Inexperienced Secretary	Helen Brooks
Ruthlessly Bedded, Forcibly Wedded	Abby Green
The Desert King's Bejewelled Bride	Sabrina Philips
Bought: For His Convenience or Pleasure?	Maggie Cox
The Playboy of Pengarroth Hall	Susanne James
The Santorini Marriage Bargain	Margaret Mayo
The Brooding Frenchman's Proposal	Rebecca Winters
His L.A. Cinderella	Trish Wylie
Dating the Rebel Tycoon	Ally Blake
Her Baby Wish	Patricia Thayer
The Sicilian's Bride	Carol Grace
Always the Bridesmaid	Nina Harrington
The Valtieri Marriage Deal	Caroline Anderson
Surgeon Boss, Bachelor Dad	Lucy Clark

HISTORICAL

The Notorious Mr Hurst	Louise Allen
Runaway Lady	Claire Thornton
The Wicked Lord Rasenby	Marguerite Kaye

MEDICAL™

The Rebel and the Baby Doctor	Joanna Neil
The Country Doctor's Daughter	Gill Sanderson
The Greek Doctor's Proposal	Molly Evans
Single Father: Wife and Mother Wanted	Sharon Archer

Pure reading pleasure™

MAY 2009 LARGE PRINT TITLES

ROMANCE

The Billionaire's Bride of Vengeance	Miranda Lee
The Santangeli Marriage	Sara Craven
The Spaniard's Virgin Housekeeper	Diana Hamilton
The Greek Tycoon's Reluctant Bride	Kate Hewitt
Nanny to the Billionaire's Son	Barbara McMahon
Cinderella and the Sheikh	Natasha Oakley
Promoted: Secretary to Bride!	Jennie Adams
The Black Sheep's Proposal	Patricia Thayer

HISTORICAL

The Captain's Forbidden Miss	Margaret McPhee
The Earl and the Hoyden	Mary Nichols
From Governess to Society Bride	Helen Dickson

MEDICAL™

Dr Devereux's Proposal	Margaret McDonagh
Children's Doctor, Meant-to-be Wife	Meredith Webber
Italian Doctor, Sleigh-Bell Bride	Sarah Morgan
Christmas at Willowmere	Abigail Gordon
Dr Romano's Christmas Baby	Amy Andrews
The Desert Surgeon's Secret Son	Olivia Gates